Captain Nemo's
Library

Other works by Per Olov Enquist
published by Quartet Books

Downfall
The Magnetist's Fifth Winter

Captain Nemo's Library

Per Olov Enquist

Translated from the Swedish

by Anna Paterson

Quartet Books

First published in Great Britain
by Quartet Books Limited 1992
A member of the Namara Group
27/29 Goodge Street
London W1P 1FD

Copyright © by Per Olov Enquist 1991
Translation copyright © by Anna Paterson 1992

Originally published under the title
Kapten Nemos bibliotek by
Norstedts Förlag, Stockholm

The Publishers are grateful to The Swedish Institute
for its support in the preparation of this translation

A catalogue record for this
book is available from the
British Library
ISBN 0 7043 7019 0

Phototypeset by Intype, London

Printed and bound in Great Britain by
Bookcraft Ltd, Midsomer Norton, Avon

TRANSLATOR'S NOTE

Per Olov Enquist's language is entirely controlled, and however unusual its structure might seem at first, working with it makes one realize just how carefully the effects are planned. The book is hard to read in the original, with sharp shifts in tone and syntax and sudden movements from standard vocabulary to distant dialect.

Some of these difficulties have been made less obtrusive in the translation, but problems of exact meaning still exist, as in the original, at several levels. One is caused by the slightly dreamlike quality of the narrative. Another is that of the dialect, which has been rendered as Scots. Some words may be hard to understand, for instance:

chiffin – particle, fragment
cleg – gadfly, horsefly
cloot – piece of cloth, rag
girn – complain peevishly, whine, grumble
greet – cry, weep
jonsie – jolly, hearty; buxom
leen – hay meadow
pech – puff, pant, gasp for breath
quaens – women
trachle – trail, walk slowly and wearily

PROLOGUE
(The last five proposals)

I

Now, soon, my benefactor, Captain Nemo, will tell me to open the ballast tanks so that the vessel, with its enclosed library, sinks.

I have gone through the library, though not all of it. I used to have secret dreams about making it all add up, so that everything would be accounted for, brought to a close. At last to be able to say: it was like this, it happened this way, this is the whole story.

But that would be contrary to better knowledge. Contrary to better knowledge is a good way to keep going. If we knew better, we would give up.

Surely there is nothing wrong in being scared and saying *now*, *soon* the whole time. It is worse when it is all over, and has become *then*, *never*. Anyway it is too late to be scared then.

Josefina Marklund visited me only once during the years

I was detained, when I stayed silent about what had really happened, the four years and two months when I said nothing though I had plenty to say. One can always get on with adding things up, while staying silent. However, she did visit me. Three months later she was dead, and the green house sold.

It was rather one-sided. She did most of the talking. She got round to Eeva-Lisa and said that she had hoped for so much when she came. She had hoped, yes. As if Eeva-Lisa, though she was a child, could be like a mother to her. Although she was the mother. Something like that, anyway, but in different words. But then, in the end, it had just been a disaster. Then she clammed up.

Not a word about her hoping to take care of the deadboy. Well, there you are. There you are.

If one cannot come out with it, it is *then*, *never*. And one just sits there, crying.

When she left I noticed that she thought to stroke my cheek, or something, but then thought maybe it was unnecessary.

When one remembers all the things that did not happen because they were unnecessary. I ought to have looked after her too.

II

Stiffness and tears. Stiffness and tears.

It was hammered into me first. Then Johannes, then Eeva-Lisa. Josefina hammered into us all that God was the punishing father, he was not 'as if' the punishing father, no, the message was that fathers here on earth were just the same. Though they were absent or dead, but still somehow threatening just because of their absence, she insisted that this was the nature of fathers. All fathers. God was the ultimate father. Punishing.

There was hope after all. Hope was the Son of Man. He was not as bad, almost wicked, the way God was. The Son of Man was bonnie and generally liked and had a wound in his side, out of which poured blood and water, and where the wretches could hide, as if in a cave, concealed from the enemy.

This was the general feeling in the village too. 'Then out thereof came blood and water'. Each prayer finished with the words 'For the sake of the blood, Amen'.

Jesus interceded with the punishing God. My whole childhood passed before I realized that the Son of Man is usually short of time. Only very rarely. And in any case, he was not with us those last sixteen days and nights, with Eeva-Lisa and me, in the cave of the dead cats.

Johannes was given a foster sister as a reward, as a kind of gift to make amends, to him was given but not to me.

This was odd. He surely thought that he would turn out to deserve such a precious gift. But there is no need to earn the most precious things. Those who are beautiful, clever and bonnie make themselves deserving, but the others may still get the most precious gifts, quite undeservedly.

It was the Benefactor, Captain Nemo, who directed me to *Nautilus*, to Johannes and to the library.

Obviously, Johannes lied the whole time. Of course he was afraid as well. But I learnt more from his lies than from his truths. The truths were always uninteresting. But when he lied he moved in very close. He left me the lies as some kind of apology. A plea for forgiveness. As if one could ask oneself for forgiveness.

Well yes, I suppose one can. Perhaps that is just what one keeps doing all the time.

Generally, when he lies he is trying to hide something important. That is the rule.

Without a name one is No one. There is some sort of liberation in this.

The last text written by Johannes, before he died on the kitchen sofa in *Nautilus* with his finka uneaten and the whole kitchen in a mess and the fleecyboots forgotten in the lobby, was an attempt to reconstruct how Eeva-Lisa came to be sent away. He made up several versions. Not so much reconstructions, spells rather.

'How she was taken away from me,' I take note of the slightly solemn tone.

Josefina Marklund, whom he always calls 'my mother', as if it was an incantation, though he knew she was mine, she had stood at the top of the stairs to the first floor and spoken furiously downwards at Eeva-Lisa. Like that, 'downwards', like a punishing God. Apparently, that was just the impression Johannes wanted to give. And at the bottom of the stairs, there he himself had been standing, witnessing.

He is always careful about places. The stairs, the outbuildings, the rooms, the wild-rose hedge, the cold spring. Down to just about every nail. When he speaks of people he lies all the time. Nails, radiators and animals on the other hand he describes with passionate truthfulness.

Still, it is a start.

The stairs recur often. And the bedroom with the fire-escape, fixed in place by Dad when the house was built, and the rowan, which was a lucky tree, in the winter it had snow on it, and birds. And the attic, where Eeva-Lisa's bed was in the summer.

The attic was untidy, and in the far corner was a cubby-hole full of old newspapers. Mostly years of copies of the *Norra Västerbotten*. They were carried along to the shit-house when it had run out of papers. The *Norrie* could also be used for wrapping things in, and for carrying the wrapped-up thing. Fish, for instance, and things like that, for throwing into the lake.

The sugar-loaf was there too. It stood on a sheet of greaseproof paper, and next to it the sugar-tongs.

Whatever he felt most unsure about, he entered into his diary, with numbers and everything. Perhaps it made him feel more secure.

Thus, according to what he states, Eeva-Lisa's mother was called Backman. She 'was born in Nyland, trained as a concert pianist in Berlin between the wars, and may have had some Walloon or tinker blood. She led a rather dubious life, and in the end again came to the notice of the local police authority when, severely ill with Parkinson's, she had been eaten by rats in Misiones, in northern Argentina.'

This is the position he takes.

He describes the death of Mrs Backman as something which happened very far away. Unable to move, eaten by rats. 'And so, at last, the first star glowed on her cheek.'

Very likely. But this is the traitor's treacherous way of avoiding the admission that something is happening nearby, not in distant Misiones, in northern Argentina.

He writes often about the sugar-loaf.

Josefina had taken him and Eeva-Lisa into the kitchen, and they had lined up, on either side of Eeva-Lisa, kneeling in front of the kitchen sofa. Time for worship and punishment in front of the loving God.

For her, who had sinned.

It was quite unimportant, he writes, a minor theft, maybe a ten-penny piece. But of course, one must pray that the contagion of sin should not spread to the beloved son, who had been found safe again and brought back into the home, not rejected, like me. Josefina wanted united prayers, united, that is, with herself, to ensure that the contagion of sin should not spread to Johannes, not drag him into that black dizzying hole of sinfulness, like the darkest deepest reaches of the oceans.

He is very informative about this expulsion of demons.

Afterwards, they sang something from the Songs of Zion. Eeva-Lisa, the sinner, sang along, but was generally quiet. For the sake of the blood, Amen.

Later on, in the evening, Johannes went to her in the attic.

It was summer-time. Outside the window was the slope with the aspens. They were gigantic, and grew like weeds, shivering as if a volcano slept its heavy sleep underground: that too was natural and understandable to us children. Volcanos always sleep. The aspens knew that they were there, they had much better hearing than people. More like cats, really.

He had gone to her in the attic, whispered her name. She did not speak. He had sat down on the edge of the bed. Her eyes were dark, holding him steadily. It was as if by looking at him without wavering, she wanted to find an answer, or ask for something, but the eyes were watchful too. 'As if I had been a messenger from Josefina, the woman who hated her so much, and whom she called mother, but who was her deadly enemy.'

This is what he writes. This is how all his writings in the library of *Nautilus* are merciful incantations. But I do not let myself be deceived any more.

Her eyes dark, her hair dark, the nails bitten. I know he loved her.

She breathed without a sound, staying silent. Then he held out his hand, offered her the lump of sugar. She did not move, did not take it. He waited, with his hand held out.

Outside in the summer night the leaves of the aspens moved softly, not to warn, but anxiously. But he writes only of Eeva-Lisa's eyes.

He knew the question. He held out his hand. Almost imperceptibly she turned her head away from him. Then he moved the lump of sugar closer, held it close, close to her mouth. Her lips were dry, slightly bitten, she breathed soundlessly. He held the lump of sugar-loaf close, close to her lips.

Then, at last he saw her lips quietly open, not much but enough for him to see; with the very tip of her tongue she cautiously touched the harsh white surface of the sugar.

There are only three kinds of people: the executioners, the victims and the traitors.

The executioners and the victims are of course quite easy to understand. The traitors have a worse time. I sometimes think that everyone should be forced to be a traitor just once. Then we would understand more

9

about those most outcast of wretches. They have the hardest time of all. But if one had been like them, one would know better what human beings are like and so be able to defend them.

III

Six months after Johannes and I were born Dad died, that is the man who was the father of at least one of us.

It was thought to be his appendix. But it was something else, an inherited illness, porphyria, which really existed only in the villages in Upper Norrland. It was heritable, it was an internal thin rootfibre of death running between families. Since the illness was so rare, it was always thought to be appendicitis, and so they prescribed medicines and carried out operations: when the illness was porphyria, almost always with fatal consequences.

He was the one who had built the green-painted house, and put up the fire-escape.

One of us, either Johannes or me, bore the imprint of the illness inside. Both of us wanted that imprint. It was the inheritance of death, which would make us live. There are many who do not know who their father is. But a mother who does not know if her child is really hers – that is unusual.

Things became a little unusual for Johannes and me too, I suppose.

This is how odd things get when one is exchanged. One has nothing, except the hope of at least having inherited an illness, death's small imprint on life, to help us survive. The most modest of heirlooms, the strange little illness, which forms a link between us, though life has tried to keep us apart.

I must be careful. Ever since I found Johannes again, in the underwater vessel, my life too has actually been at risk.

The incident on the staircase took place in December 1944. I happen to know this, precisely. Eeva-Lisa was taken away from him then.

She was to be sent away.

Everything painless is recorded, from the shape of the staircase to the position of the pissbucket. And how she screamed down at Eeva-Lisa that she had to go.

But not why. It is unimaginable that he does not see that Josefina Marklund is terribly, unbearably afraid. Unbelievable that anyone can be so blind, unable to see that raisin-like face contracted with fear.

The tone of the writing, as he lies about her, is noticeably not the right one.

Now, soon.

Nothing wrong with being afraid, I suppose. Everybody is of course. Then, one says *now*, *soon*, and hopes secretly that it might be too late.

I have travelled far since what happened that time with Eeva-Lisa, and the sixteen days and nights with her in the cave of the dead cats. Many years have passed, and I have caused myself some pain, hurt others too. When I thought of Johannes and Eeva-Lisa and me, for a long time it was like a sharp, burning point of pain, a grain of sand in an eye, and it took me almost a whole lifetime to realize that it was that small pain which reassured me that I was alive. And that I was still somehow a human being.

Rejecting that pain would have made it meaningless. Then it would just have hurt.

He sends me signals by way of his untidy little notes from the library. I found them everywhere in *Nautilus*.

I have collected them.

'Breathe forth my face.'

'One must be grateful towards one's benefactors, otherwise one must feel shame and guilt.'

Shame, and guilt.

But I know he loved her. And when it had become too late, and the first star had already begun to glow on her cheek, nothing remained for him but to immure himself in Captain Nemo's library to reconstruct his magic spells.

We discovered the cave of the dead cats the same day we killed the baby birds. It was the year before the exchange, and Johannes was still my best friend.

We had found a bird's nest up in the forest, near the path leading to the top of Benshill. We found the nest on the right hand side as you come up. Then, fifty metres further along, we discovered the cave with the dead cats.

When I was a child, the cats behaved like elephants: they withdrew when they were about to die. We knew everything about the elephants, they withheld their deaths from the world, they hid their deaths from life. And it was just the same with our cats. In this way, death was two different things, which did not agree with each other, or maybe meant the same thing differently. On one hand, it was important to take photographs of dead people in their coffins. Corpse-pictures were important. Then the pictures had to be framed and put on the chest of drawers in the parlour behind the kitchen. Then one could compare one-self with the dead, with one's father for instance, and turn almost as cold as ice if the picture was just like oneself. But then everything was also put into order and rightness, and one was part of the corpse. But at the same time death was meant to be like a dying elephant. One withdrew from life and died, but was still alive, but detached.

Many people lived like that.

The bird's nest was close to the crest of the hill, where the elk watchtower was. The eggs had just hatched, the fledglings were alive and their mouths were constantly open. They demanded the whole time, but we had nothing. Still, we thought they were bonnie, and wanted to put leaves on top, almost like a sheepskin cover, against the cold at night, so that they should not get a chill.

They were a little sticky to touch.

We went back two days later. The leaves were still there, untouched. We picked them off. The fledglings were dead. They had not realized that we were benefactors. They had been left behind, because human beings have some kind of deadly smell.

There was nothing we could do. We had murdered the baby birds. We had marked them with the human odour of death.

I remember that we were upset. The Mummy-bird had simply left them. It was the year before the exchange, and Johannes was still my best friend and had not moved into the green house.

The same day we discovered the cave of the dead cats.

I did not have a single book when I was a child, but after the exchange Johannes got twelve, and he gave me one. It was *The Mysterious Island*.

Throughout our childhood we learnt to follow up clues and to send signals. *The Mysterious Island* was a signal. The problem was how to interpret it. It took almost a whole lifetime, but in the end I could do it.

The important thing was the death-camp of the Benefactor. The Benefactor, who called himself Captain Nemo, had made his last camp in the centre of the Franklin volcano. He had time for the settlers on the island, the half-blind, the fallen, those who scarcely believed themselves human. The Son of Man was an ideal, but never had the time. The Benefactor could be trusted.

Everything would have been so simple, if I had understood from the beginning. Johannes would wait for me in the library on board *Nautilus*. Captain Nemo would guide me. There, at last, I would be able to sum things up, open the ballast tanks and row away.

The story is about Johannes and Eeva-Lisa and me and Alfhild and Mum in the green house. But I understood it first after having found Johannes again, in Captain Nemo's library.

This is how it came about.

Franklin Island was off the coast of Nyland.

Captain Nemo had left instructions. I was simply to follow the thin metal wire, through the partly collapsed tunnel leading through to the crater.

This was in the book. It was easy.

The thin wire disappeared into the water. I anchored the boat next to the rock, it tapped against the mountain in the sea like a bird's beak, but not a second of eternity would have passed even if I had stayed there for ever. This is how it was, the human relationship with God: God was the terrifying eternity, but the task of the human being was to wear away the mountain of eternity with his bird's beak, to reach the Benefactor. This was how I had learnt to see it when I was a child.

God was something hard and enormous that was called eternity. And man was something small and stubborn, with a bird's beak, who would one day reduce God to nothing, God that was the black mountain in the sea. It was incredible, hardly possible. But then, one must keep trying. No wonder that a human wretch needed help and guidance from a benefactor in this hopeless battle against God.

The flood tide covered the mouth of the cave. I had to wait. Then the tide would retreat, and the entrance to the cave be freed.

I sat under a projecting piece of rock. It rained, a storm came and went, silence fell, I watched the water flowing away. I thought that soon it would be explained to me. One cannot explain love. But if the mountain in the sea that is God can be reduced to nothing, and this makes one human, then surely love too can be explained?

I climbed into the boat again, and began rowing towards the centre of the volcanic crater.

The cave gradually grew wider. Finally I could see all of it.

The roof of the cave was a vault about thirty metres high. It was a gigantic cave, an immense subterranean cathedral, where the roof gleamed pale blue, mingling with soft shades of reddish white, it rose in an immense arch over the sea, which covered the floor of the cave: it was like entering the inside of a human being.

In the human belly, that was where I was. As if in my own insides: I observed the very simplest secret of the riddle from the inside, where it had always been, but where it could not have been expected.

The roof of the cave seemed to be supported by pillars, tens, maybe hundreds of almost identical pillars shaped by nature alone: perhaps as early as when the earth was formed. I liked to think that the earth had been made in a single action, created suddenly, as if in an act of love.

These basalt pillars stood with their bases in the shining still surface of the water, sunk into the black water, which was like mercury: yes, that is how the water seemed to me, like shining black mercury, it was not connected to the sea round the island, instead it had chosen to be still and to stay unmoved by the storms of life. In here it was so still. This channel of mercury wanted to be still like this.

Like an arm of black water, rising up through the centre of the volcano, a giant's black arm extending in the centre of life.

In the centre of life.

I let the boat slowly glide forward and stop. And then I saw the vessel there, in the centre.

Light came from the deck of the vessel, there were two sources of light, maybe two floodlights. The shafts of light were at first united and concentrated, and powerful, but later scattered a little. The light bounced against the walls of the cave, turning the stone formations into crystals; innumerable reflections which did not illuminate the roof of the cave. The water, black mercury. I floated there in stillness, with the vessel a hundred metres away. And the reflected lights, like stars up there, thirty metres up.

It was like late winter nights in my childhood. At that time the northern lights still flared in the sky. It was before the northern lights were taken away from us, and while the stars were still thin and warm and piercing. One could stay out in the snow and look up towards the light signals high up: a world populated by the black star-holes and the wires coming from the stars. Johannes, before he became a traitor, had said that this was the heavenly harp. On cold winter nights you could hear the music, when the secret world he and I had created would be singing: nights full of stars and wires and music and secret signals. All this served to indicate the secret routes into Franklin cave, where our benefactor was still hidden, the one who would guide us in the end and make everything fit together, make everything add up, everything add up at last. It was a world of secret signs which had been entrusted to us, and nobody was left behind.

Now I knew that he was here. Under the false stars created by the floodlights. It was to this place he had withdrawn. It was to this place he had made me come, as he had once promised he would.

The two floodlights were one cable's length away. I started rowing.

I turned and looked at the vessel, which by now I could see very clearly.

It floated in the centre of the volcanic cave, supported

17

by the enormous black arm of mercury, a very long, spindle-shaped black object. It was about ninety metres long, and projected some three to four metres above the surface of the water. I could not establish with certainty the physical composition of the vessel, but its material was not wood, rather metal of some kind, aluminium or black steel.

My boat was gliding slowly towards the vessel. I recognized it easily. It was a ship and was so exactly like the illustrations in the book Johannes had given me that it must be just the one I had seen, and that he had dreamt of.

I was gliding towards the left side of the ship. Everything had been properly prepared. The ship's hull was made of black metal. I moored my boat and climbed up. A hatch in the middle of the deck was waiting, opened.

So I started climbing down into the interior of the submarine.

At first he had no books at all. Then he began to read the books in Sehlstedt's box, where the Blue Ribbon Library books were kept. When they realized that he liked reading, he was given his first book. Later, until the incident with Eeva-Lisa in the woodshed, he was given a total of twelve books.

Giving me that particular one of the twelve – *The Mysterious Island* by Jules Verne – was no coincidence. He could have given me *The Cave Mystery* (about an adventure in the Pays Basque with pelota and involving a cave deeper than that of the cats) or Kipling's *Kim*, which I read so many times that in the end I stopped understanding it, and only knew that one day I too would be immersed in a river of insights, if I waited long enough. Or Mia Hallesby's

18

Three Hundred Tales for Children. It contained the story about the gigantic black mountain in the sea, and the bird that flew there once every thousand years to sharpen its beak. And when the ten-miles-long, ten-miles-wide and ten-miles-high mountain had been completely worn away, one second of eternity would have passed. This was the dream of man's battle with God. But it was dreadful.

Some nights I could not sleep, because this immense eternity filled me with such terror. Yes, perhaps that is how it was, that his very small library of twelve books in reality shaped my world, that the fairy tales, images and terrifying fantasies got established then, and remained unchanged. But for a long time I was quite sure how it would end: I would be guided to the ultimate library, where the myths would be replaced by clarity, anguish by explanations, and where everything at last would be made to fit together.

He told me later that at first, for some time, he had *Robinson Crusoe* in mind, a book he worked at for many years ('worked' was one of his favourite words, when something had captured his imagination) and from which I have seen him copy innumerable times the endless lists of items salvaged from the shipwreck; write them down and extend them, as if these lists ('four flint-locks, one barrel gunpowder, eight pounds dried goat's meat, five axes, five handaxes') had been incantations, calming rituals, and objects which he, like the solitary man on the island, could keep safely in his cave, and so feel secure against the world.

But he gave me another book.

He decided on *The Mysterious Island*, and in it he marked with a line the very end, which deals with the discovery in the library of the Benefactor, immured in the ship.

That is how I came to find him.

By the way: it is not true that I once loved Eeva-Lisa.

It is not true. At least, if I did it was a very strange love. Faced with that one must surely feel ashamed, and guilty.

I climbed down into the shaft, carefully closing the hatch behind me, as if I wanted to prepare for departure, though of course I knew better.

Below the flight of steps stretched a long, narrow passage. It was lit by electricity, and there was a door at the end of it. I went up to the door. I opened it.

I was in a vast drawing-room. A museum, so extensive and huge that not even as a child, when I spoke like a child and dreamed a child's dreams, could I ever have imagined it. In this museum were collected all the mineral treasures of the world. But in here was also part of the treasure from the stranded ship, items entered on the salvage lists. He had included all the objects on his salvage lists, those he had copied and those he had extended; and so carefully had he noted everything down that now it could all be found in this place, his last museum.

But then I knew Johannes so well. Here in the museum, he had at last managed to bring everything together, for real: the barrels of gunpowder, the dried reindeer-meat, the barrels of salt, molasses, flintlocks, the five handaxes. Everything was the way it should be. Displayed in this museum.

I looked for a long time, without surprise, at the familiar objects. I crossed the floor to the wall where the axes were hanging. I recalled the word 'testingly' and slid my finger

20

testingly along the edge of an axe. I thought for a while about the cave of the dead cats and smiled, testingly but sadly.

Then I opened the door and went in. And there was the library.

He was lying on a bed, asleep, and he had not heard me. I recognized the couch. It was the kitchen sofa.

Captain Nemo had shown me the right way. I had found Johannes again.

I went up to him. He was sleeping in his library, and he had waited for a long time. He slept lightly, like a bird, lips slightly parted, a light, soundless, childlike sleep. It was as if he smiled, and every breath was like a bird's. I remembered how I had seen Johannes the time I tried to return to the house after our exchange: he had been locked up in the lobby. He was standing on the other side of the pane of glass, not allowed to speak to me, and he scratched against the windowpane with his nail, as if he wanted to leave an invisible mark. And I felt that he was like a bird, there behind the pane, a bird touching it with the tips of its wings: so inaudible had been his violent breathing, and so indistinct his crying, that I could hear only the sound of his nail against the pane, like the bird's wingtip against the window which excluded it from the freedom which suddenly I saw I embodied.

He slept now. He looked bonnie. I had never thought that this traitor could look so bonnie. But how old he had become. As old as me. How old had I become myself then.

– Johannes, I said in a quiet voice. Johannes, it is me. Now I am here.

Then his breathing changed its pattern: he stepped out of his dream, opened his eyes.

How old he had become. We observed each other in silence. He said nothing. Once more I said:

– Johannes?

I thought perhaps he had not heard me the first time. But I am sure he did.

Now he was old. He looked quite bonnie. His library was all around him. No longer twelve books, as it was once, when he gave me one of them. There were hundreds, maybe thousands of books. I knew immediately that he had written them all. As he had promised once when we were young, he had immured himself in his library.

And he turned with such a bonnie smile and said:

– Guid God, ye've come hame tae gie's a visit.

The ship was a submarine. It was called *Nautilus*.

This is how we had planned it together.

Then, we had been dreaming how in the end everything would be just like the last descent of Captain Nemo. He was to die confined within the crater of the volcano. The submarine's waterpumps would slowly and solemnly be opened by me, and as the last visitor, I would then leave the vessel. The ballast tanks would fill. And the descent begin. Only the hermetically sealed library would last, with all its doors welded shut, the library containing all that would be lost, the final reports and the speeches for the defence. And while the floodlights were still lit, the submarine called *Nautilus* would slowly sink into the water-filled crater of the volcano. There, even after the last glimpse of the light from the floodlights had disappeared, he would continue to live in the innermost merciful darkness. There his coffin, the fantastic submarine, would surround him, he would be dead but living, without air and without food and without pain, for eternity's eternity.

That is how we imagined it at the time, how we had planned it: to live without pain, forever deep down in Captain Nemo's library.

There was no need for us to say anything special, so we stayed silent.

An hour later he fell asleep again. I realized that he was ill and would die soon.

Morning came.

I saw it, not however by any light penetrating the circular windows. No light entered the cave of course. No, I was watching his clock, which had once hung in the kitchen, and which his father had bought before his death. The clock had a hand which moved very slowly, so that one full turn corresponded not to twelve hours, but to twenty-four. This way, the middle of the day, twelve o'clock, was at the lowermost point of the clockface, and morning was out sideways, on the right hand side of the face.

I watched the clock without surprise, because I had seen it when I was a child.

At about eight in the morning I went into the inner room.

It was a kitchen, its cooker a skilfully fitted iron range surrounded by ingeniously decorated marble tiles, probably of Indian origin. The iron range was well made, with rings which could be removed by means of a hook. On one side was a copper urn full of water, to help maintain the right level of humidity in the air. Water from the urn could be drawn from a little tap in front.

The range burned wood. The fire had gone out.

He had put a pan on the range. It was half-full of food. I went up to the cooker and looked at the contents of the frying-pan. It was familiar. It was finka. Finka is made from hard, quite substantial flatbread, it is broken up into small inch-long pieces and fried in melted butter, with some milk poured on, a quarter of a litre or thereabouts. I knew he had always been fond of finka, which he often ate with some herring, or at other times, just with a pat of butter.

I took the frying-pan, and poured the rest of the finka into a soup-plate. Then I ate it, without reheating it. It was just as nice anyway. With it, I drank a glass of small beer.

Then I went back.

I remember that we were both very fond of finka.

He slept more deeply now.

I put my hand on his forehead, it was sweaty. He turned uneasily in his sleep, but did not wake up.

I looked around the library. I knew I was to stay here for a while.

Lying on the floor was the very last text he had been working at. I read it. There were only a few lines.

I can still see the house in front of me, with its quite steep staircase leading down to the road towards the woodplaner's plant. Below the leens ran a burn, crossed by a road. Near this little bridge was a jetty. At the time which I now recall, I was three or four years old.

I was on all fours on the jetty, poking with a stick in the mud where the black leeches were, and I remember how, for the first time, I was roused to insight into my own life. I clearly remember how I suddenly looked up, and shamefully dried my hands, and how I thought: if somebody was to see you here . . . then . . . then you should feel ashamed of yourself. I often lay on my jetty, looking into the water, watching the black leeches, maybe they were horse leeches, swimming up towards me with long sinuous movements, swerve and return down to the mud. I could not understand what they were searching for in the mud, I assumed that they wanted to get washed clean by taking their long swims. And in order to help them as best I could, I pulled these blood-sucking leeches, I later learnt they were horse leeches, out from the mud, where, all curled up, they clung to their black mire bed, and lifted them up on to the jetty. I then washed these creatures from the burn so carefully, so lovingly that in the end they became utterly. . . . clean.

At this point he seems to have paused, ruled out the last lines, as if after closer thought, and then come back to a quite different event, which apparently took place at a much later date.

That passage, in its entirety, runs as follows – it describes the incident on the stairs:

We were on our way up to the attic when my mother stopped us.

Eeva-Lisa had got about ten steps up, maybe fewer,

and I was at the bottom, I had not even put my foot on the lowest step. Just then my mother began talking, and all three of us remained standing in the same place, throughout.

I could see my mother's face clearly. She had come out from the bedroom, with a severe and almost remote expression on her face, which later, as she spoke, or rather screamed, ever more loudly, changed, slowly and quite inexplicably. It was as if a wave of rage, dammed up for a long time, suddenly tore her features apart, and came close to dehumanizing her face, so that the usually severe, regular features (at other times so gentle and almost beautiful) now contracted, as if in uncontrollable spasms, almost as if in pain.

She began, using words which I understood at first, but later did not want to understand. Initially the words had recognizable meaning, the lengthy sequence of righteous judgement and perceptive accusation, which in part I had heard before, and understood, but now they merged into accusations that I did not understand, and only the impression of immense fury remained. Or hatred. Yes, suddenly I realized with dismay that she was full of hate, not the usual hatred which could be understood, but something different. And she screamed, full of hatred and fury, that Eeva-Lisa must go away now, for ever, it had all been a mistake and now she had to get out of the house.

It was then, I admit it, that I started screaming.

The next bit had a line through it, but was easily readable, and said:

I write *admit* because I distinctly remember feeling ashamed as I screamed. And I admit it *shamefully*, because it was just at that moment that I also saw something in my mother's face that I will never forget: the extreme loneliness in that face, and the fact that she was afraid.

I had never been able to believe that she could be afraid. She had never ever been afraid before. And as I screamed in desperation and terror I understood, ever more clearly, and this was to draw one period of my life to its close and catapult me into a new one, that in this moment both Eeva-Lisa and my mother would be taken away from me, in just the same way that everything had been taken away from me once before when I was exchanged, and that Eeva-Lisa and my mother would leave me behind, like an empty snail's shell, and nothing could ever give them back to me. And later I would realize that this was a stage in my life which would be repeated again and again, a stage of abandonment and deprivation.

She had spoken down at Eeva-Lisa and me. Then I started screaming. And suddenly Josefina realized that from this moment, she herself would also become utterly alone.

Never, never will I be able to free myself from this moment. However long I live it will be with the knowledge that death visited me that moment, the hands of the clock pointing to twenty-four, but stopped. This was how Eeva-Lisa left me, but also how my mother was abandoned at last. I saw her face as she turned to me. And afterwards I had thought: How strange that a powerful and punitive God can be so fearful of abandonment.

Though at the time it was Eeva-Lisa who was mostly in my thoughts, I ought to have thought of my mother. Her face became like the bird's nest, when one takes away the leaves covering the nest, and finds the dead fledglings, suddenly there, in death and loneliness.

This is what happened when they were taken away from me.'

I must have been reading for hours. Fell asleep, on a bed in the room next to the library in *Nautilus*.

This room was quite different from the museum room and the library, very untidy, barely furnished. I recognized the cubbyhole, half nailed shut in a corner, where the old newspapers were kept, back copies of the local paper *Norra Västerbotten*.

I was lying on an old sheepskin which I had pulled round me. I got the idea that it was the same skin that had covered grandmother when she died, but rejected the thought, since that skin could not very well be here inside the submarine *Nautilus*: of course, it had been handed on to Nicanor Markström from Oppstoppet.

I went into the library.

The clock on the wall, the one with a twenty-four-hour clockface, not a twelve-hour one, seemed to have moved on, perhaps a few turns, but I could no longer be sure if it was morning or evening. It did not matter. The precision I had striven for previously had made me prisoner of the clock. Now I was free, now I was just a prisoner of the library and of Johannes.

In this way I had at last become imprisoned by myself.

I went up to him. His eyes were closed. His forehead was damp, he moaned feebly, and I realized that he was suffering pains in his sleep.

His mouth was half open. One hand moved as if in spasms. I tried to relax his fingers, so that he would not hurt himself, but he seemed to be very strong still.

He was ill and in pain. I realized that he would die very soon.

He had often written about the stages of pain, in his messages to me. What he experienced now were physical pains: one might live or die enduring them, but without real hurt. The internal stages of pain he had catalogued here in his library; here, in this library soon to be immersed in the interior of the volcano.

I fetched a blanket and put it over him. Gradually he moved more calmly, in the end lying quite still as if the pain had left him for a while. His hand opened up, the spasms loosened their grip.

I really ought to have started my work with the library, but could not get round to it. I just sat there, watching him.

Soon Johannes would die. At last.

I must have fallen asleep in my chair.

Woke, read for a few hours. He was moaning again. I tried to give him some water, but he did not want to drink.

He had always looked bonnie. That is the word they used for him when he was little. But how old he had become.

I think he recognized me. Because he had asked if it was me. If I had come home to visit him.

And then surely I must have been the one who had come home.

I remember the sun-clock on the floor in the cave of the dead cats.

Captain Nemo had taken care of the kitchen clock from the green house and kept it here, in the submarine.

The clock on the wall moved, no, not the clock, but the hands, so I assume that time passed. Every time the hands pointed straight up it was night. Then the clock mimicked the moment that had been, a day and a night earlier: it could have been now. But the clock had no memory, it could not remember the twenty-four hours, only the second that was now.

This brief eternal second was of course in reality quite useless. It had no memory. Johannes and I did though, and so did our library.

Sometimes I could feel a slight shiver running through the hull of *Nautilus*, as if deep down there the volcano had sleepily turned over, and then gone back to sleep again.

I wonder if volcanoes can feel pain while they sleep, in the moment before they are to wake and die.

'The cave of the dead cats' he had written in the margin of one of the pages.

Like a small plea to me.

V

Now, soon.

I

THE INTRUDERS IN THE GREEN HOUSE

1

THE ARRIVAL OF THE SETTLERS

Big sister Eeva-Lisa, she
   had a bastard in time for tea.
Scared of Mum and of God she had lain,
   scared of the fish and of Jesu bad pain.

In the dark she hid her shame
   to the outhouse-door she came.
No key, all shut, and she pulled it in vain.
No God in the shed and her alone with her pain.

I

The right to live in the green house came to belong to me, because of a mistake made at the hospital in Bureå in September 1934, the day Johannes and I were born.

Later the mistake was corrected. Then I was exchanged, according to proper legal procedure, and the right to live in the green house taken away from me. Instead it was bestowed upon Johannes Marklund.

Later still, Eeva-Lisa was bestowed upon him, to replace me. As a result of his treachery she was taken away from him, and therefore taken away from me. Johannes took over the rights to the green house, became a traitor, had her taken away from him, and lost his rights to the house as well. Three years later the house burnt down. This is a brief summary of the whole story.

'The pulse-beats of death' Johannes wrote in a note to me.

I thought at first that he was talking about an approaching physical death. But I now believe that he meant something quite different.

He meant: that I must realize that nothing is hopeless, not even death, and that it is even possible to rise again in this life on earth, like Eeva-Lisa, simply by not continuing to exist as dead.

Woke at three forty-five, the dream about the cave of the dead cats was still very real. Unintentionally stroked my face with a finger, against the skin of the cheek.

Had been very close to the answer.

Out there, above the water, hung a strange morning mist: the darkness had lifted, but a hovering grey cloudiness was still there, not white but somehow reflecting darkness; it hovered about ten metres above the surface of the water which was absolutely still and shiny, like mercury. The birds slept, tightly wrapped in their dreams. I could imagine myself on the outermost shore, and in front of me nothingness.

An outermost boundary. But also the birds, wrapped tightly in their dreams.

34

Suddenly, a movement: a bird taking off. I heard no sound, just saw it beat the surface with the tips of its wings, free itself, rise upwards at an angle: it happened suddenly, and so lightly, so weightlessly. I saw how it took off and rose up towards the grey ceiling of mist, and vanished. And I had heard no sound.

That must have been how she died. Not like the sound of snails getting crushed under my feet. But lightly, the way a bird takes off and rises and is suddenly gone. And it is quite certain that it will descend through the mist again, down towards the water, and return, somehow, but for certain.

II

Already on the second day Eeva-Lisa was told, over the breakfast porridge, to call Josefina Mum.

She obeyed at once. At that time I had been exiled from the house for a year.

For a long time I believed that there was only one true line in the ballad he was hiding in the library, and which I had retrieved: 'Scared of Mum, scared of the fish'.

The fish was easy for me to understand of course. But Mum?

There was much said about the outbuildings in his speech for the defence. Very little about Mum. He shifted the outbuildings around, to frighten me, but described them in great detail, to calm me down.

I feel calm. But then it rarely helps to be calm.

However: it was typical of him to try to come closer by writing verses.

Presumably, he was trying to get me into a friendly mood. Verse, like poetry, was a sin of course, practically a mortal sin. It was sinful to write verses, unless they were for hymns. Almost anything could be said in verse form. So they were necessary, but also a bit unnecessary. And there was no need to ascribe any truth to them.

The saga about the notebook is one he constantly repeats. Thus: Dad had a notebook in which he wrote down verses. That is to say, poetry. He was supposed to have written it down after he came home from the forest, in the evenings. Or on Sundays, which was less likely, or at least more sinful. To write verses on a Sunday must be twice the sin, except on Good Friday, when it was mortal sin.

Josefina had told him that she had burnt the notebook. He would not have to show it to the Creator on Judgement Day.

But of course neither she nor Johannes knew that one night Captain Nemo had come to me and Eeva-Lisa, in the cave of the dead cats, and given me the notebook with the verses.

I will come back to the exchange. First of all I am now going to recount what happened when Eeva-Lisa arrived for my best friend, Johannes, the victorious conqueror, generally so well liked, the one who would later betray Eeva-Lisa.

Johannes had caused problems after being handed over on 4 December 1940.

He had seemed a bit nervous ever since he had been carried there by the police, and I had been carried away. On the other hand, he was well looked after. But still, Josefina explained, he seemed a little nervous. Nobody asked if it was she who had become nervous. It was Johannes. The vicar too had been tenderhearted. This was why it was decided that he should have a foster sister. One could of course have imagined a foster brother, me for instance, but justice must be done, and Sven Hedman, who had lost Johannes through the court's decision, and had to make do with me, felt silent at heart at the mere thought. And so the foster sister arrived.

I am describing this completely without bitterness.

When she arrived, Johannes was sitting at the kitchen window, where I used to sit, looking out over the hillside. It was September 1941. The birches still had a few yellow leaves clinging to them, but it had snowed overnight; and now it was as if the snow rested on the yellow leaves, touched them, lightly, like the kiss of death. It was that very ordinary, very brief moment, which always hurts a little: autumn was at its most beautiful and most threatening then. The next day the snow would be gone, and when the snow disappeared the leaves would go too. But just that day the colours and leaves and snow fitted together; death and yellow leaves and snow.

It really lasted for only a few hours. Not a long time, just a second out of a life. But when all the earlier, beautiful part was forgotten, and the later, white part too, then this remained, easy to remember, for ever.

Eeva-Lisa came from the bus, which had stopped to let people off. The driver, it was Marklin, had let her off. And she walked up towards the green house.

She had brought a suitcase.

It was quite a big thing to have one's own suitcase. Everybody in the village had backpacks, of course, but on the whole only the vicar's wife had a suitcase, she lived in

Bureå, and was thought to gi' hersel' airs and to be something the vicar should not really have to be stuck with. No
one had seen the vicar's wife's suitcase, actually, but this
is what was generally said.

That is how suitcases were thought of. Eeva-Lisa arrived
with a suitcase, but many years later, when those things
had happened, nobody could really be bothered mentioning
it. It was, everyone agreed, not worth argufying about.

But the suitcase was surely wrong. There was much that
was wrong about Eeva-Lisa right from the start.

First, the parish paid for her. Not much, in fact hardly
anything at all, Josefina always made a point of that. All
in all, it might have covered the cost of the finka, putting
it that way, but even so. Then she had a lewd mother, not
thought worth speaking about in particular, but who
besides was said to have been a piano-lady, that is someone
who played the piano. Not the organ. And then she had a
father who had taken off to South America. Or it could
have been her grandfather. Nobody was entirely sure.

And, of course, everybody was very careful not to say
that she had tinkers' blood in her veins. Because that was
just a matter for speculation.

But she had brought a suitcase. That was a bit too uppity.
Quite natural in a way, maybe, something lots of people
in the village did not think worth going on about. But it
was of course quite certain that she had brought a suitcase
when she came.

Johannes had been sitting at the kitchen window when
she came. She had a suitcase in her hand. She lugged it
along. It had snowed that night, but the leaves stayed on.
When she was almost at the door he went to sit down on

the sofa, so that she should not notice that he had been watching. It was unnecessary to appear curious.

There was much in the village that was unnecessary. Disliked things were unnecessary, in other words more or less everything. Generally, everything that was, well, how to put it, that was otherwise. In any case, it was unnecessary.

A kind of commandment which meant: no. A very short commandment. But quite important.

III

The colours were also important.

The chapel next door was yellow, but the house was green. When she came close to the green house, which was level with the yellow one, Johannes sat down on the sofa so that she would not notice. He sat there when she came in, and after he had greeted her.

It was only on the following day that she was told to say Mum.

He had been nervous ever since he had heard the news that she was coming. He had thought about it so intently that the two hours last Sunday, when James (pronounced Schamese) Lindgren had read from Rosenius, those hours had passed like the wind. James Lindgren read from Rosenius in a rather monotonous voice, until the children could bear it no more. Then he would stop and finish with a prayer, which ended 'For the sake of the blood, Amen'. It had nothing to do with slaughtering, that was understood.

There were children who could stand listening to James (pronounced Schamese) Lindgren for perhaps three hours; they were thought of as budding preachers on account of their durability. James Lindgren was widely respected, but he had a droning voice and changed his snuff every half-hour, even during Rosenius. The Sunday before Eeva-Lisa was to come, after he had been told she would, the hours in chapel had passed like the wind, so obviously he was nervous.

The altar-piece in the chapel showed Jesus, who loves all children, and its frame had a chip out of it. The chapel was yellow. The green house must have looked very pretty when she came, against the newly fallen snow and the yellow leaves.

I write about this without bitterness.

That our house was painted green we all found a little odd, since naturally most of the houses were red. But people in the village thought that one should not take it too seriously, and said nothing, at least not to Johannes and me. Besides, we were rather small and it was better to hold one's tongue. Little pitchers have big ears, and so on. Whichever way one looked at it, whether Johannes or I had the right to live in the green house, we had of course many relatives in the village. Dad had painted the house green, and then died, and one had to be respectful to the deceased. So not much was said about the colour.

The house was situated some one thousand one hundred kilometres north of Stockholm, and on the right-hand side coming from Nordmarks, or on the left-hand side coming from Koppra. It was green.

The house was up at the edge of the forest.

It had two floors, the second of which was partly furnished. At one gable end, the one with the bedroom window looking out over the burn and the valley with the lake and Hjoggböle marsh with Ryss Island, at that gable end stood a rowan tree.

It was a lucky tree.

The porch was on one of the long sides of the house, that facing the yellow chapel, which also was on the left coming from Koppra but on the right coming from Stockholm. Somebody, whose name I cannot remember, from Västra, had been to Stockholm, they had a preachers' school called Johanneslund there, that was nothing to argufy about. On that long side was the kitchen window where Johannes had been sitting waiting when Eeva-Lisa came. Down by the burn were the woodplaner's and the bloodsucking leeches. You could see straight across the lake to Sven Hedman's, which later, after the exchange, was going to be my proper home, but from Hedman's you could not see the woodplaning plant. On certain evenings, Josefina Marklund decided, the people in the green house, that is to say she and I, should get together in the kitchen and ask forgiveness for things they had done. One had to tell of some sin one had committed.

At first Josefina did not join the group, that is she was there, but did not confess. Later on she joined in. The hardest bit was to think of a sin. Then it was easy to confess. After the exchange Johannes took over with the confession, and when Eeva-Lisa arrived, she too had to join in and confess. Mum mostly confessed that she had doubted the Saviour and failed in faith, but once when I said that I had too, she got quite sharp and told me off. So next time one had to think up a real sin again, but Mum carried on confessing doubts and failures of faith. She thought it was unnecessary for her to change. Nothing to argufy about anyway. From the window one could see

41

the yellow house where the Saviour hung, and where there was a chip out of the frame of the picture.

On top of the porch was a verandah. It was quite bonnie. Hops grew there in the summer. I feel unwell. The yellow colour on the chapel is quite jarring, but nobody said anything about it. It was as if no one cared, somehow. This is strange. Once, before we were exchanged, my best friend, who was called Johannes, had fixed a clothes line to the verandah, and I had climbed down it, as if there was a great emergency; and Johannes was standing over yonder by the apple tree and helped with a brief and powerful warning shout, and then I climbed down in order to avoid the pursuers. The rope burned hot and the palms of my hands were scorched. I have got the scars still, in a way.

There was a wild-rose hedge below the house. It ran alongside the front of the house.

When we picked mushrooms it was mostly morels. They had to be poached. Afterwards, the word *poached* came to mean flesh, rotting body and death. I learnt it was a matter of dying cleanly and whitely, like a fly between the inner and outer window-panes, or the bird, not poached like a morel or like Aron Markström from Oppstoppet when they found him. Rune Renström, who was a child then, had been there and told what it was like, how Aron looked like the swollen flesh of a deid fish. Rune was my cousin, that is, if I see it the way it was before the exchange.

Dad had built the house. Before it was quite finished he planted the apple tree in the yard. The bairns from Östra came and stole the fruit; it was not very usual to have apples, but since he died young nobody bothered to say it was a bit peculiar to plant apple trees.

I cannot bear talking about Johannes's house any more now. It hurts so. Why does it hurt so much. Now I shall explain about the outbuildings.

IV

There were two more houses on the site. I am not denying that.

In the first place, then, there was the green house, which was small, but well built and painted green, and which had an inside staircase, with the pissbucket to the left at the top, that was the staircase where Eeva-Lisa was banished. The biggest of the outbuildings was really a summerhouse. Outside, at one gable-end, was an aspen that had been struck by lightning, it happened the previous winter, and I had been frightened. Dad had built that summerhouse too.

Before he died, just a month earlier, he had bought a fiddle. He had never learnt to play it. In the corpse-picture Dad looks more like me than Johannes, but then there could have been something wrong with the camera. For a long time I supposed that the fiddle had got lost, but I found it later in the ante-room to the kitchen in Captain Nemo's library in *Nautilus*, before the ballast tanks filled and I left the vessel.

I brought the fiddle with me then.

The summerhouse looked rather odd. It was sort of five-sided, due to the road, which went past the chapel up towards the hill with the cave of the dead cats, because that road was somehow squeezing itself in. So that way the summerhouse got squeezed even before it was built. People in the village did not understand this, but if something is squeezed at the beginning, it stays squeezed later on. So it becomes five-sided, for just that reason. The road was path most of the way, though quite wide. Good Friday the year before we were exchanged Johannes had come to my home, we were alone in the house, and then a Jehovah's Witness, out selling things, had been coming along the road down by the burn. We hid on the verandah, and she was left standing there knocking on the door in vain, because she had sinned by selling books on a Good Friday when the Saviour was hanging on his cross, and one was not even allowed to knit an oven-glove, even less a glove for Finland's cause, leaving the trigger-finger free, because then stillness and sorrow should rule over all mankind.

It had been quite exciting. We had been lying there quiet as mice. We were on the verandah and looked through the hop-leaves at the yellow house beyond the five-sided summerhouse and listened as she vainly knocked on the door. She was not very old and did not at all look like a Jehovah's Witness, she looked quite bonnie instead, and that evening I did not want to tell of how she had come and knocked and gone away. If she had not been a Jehovah's Witness, I often thought later on, when I lived at Sven Hedman's, then you could have opened the door and given her a piece of bake and a sugardoddle and sat for a while to hear what she might have to speak of.

The summerbothy was usually called the boat-house, because it was said to look like a boat-house, though that was something nobody had seen, except the stevedores. It was as if a boat had rammed its snout straight into the hillside. Like a stranded Ark, almost.

The question was where a Jehovah's Witness like that could have turned up from.

44

Just above the summerbothy, only ten metres further on, was the woodshed, with a shit-house built into it. The first time I came to see Johannes after the exchange he had been sitting in the shit-house, which had two holes, with one on the step for the bairns, and he was reading Popeye in the *Norrie*. And then Mum had come rushing out on to the porch with her face all twisted and asked if my Mum had allowed me to come over. Her face was all twisted, like a raisin. She looked utterly raging, as if she was going dementit. But I just steeled myself and said quite meekly that I was allowed. And then she had gone back indoors. When Johannes and I came into the kitchen later on she was sitting there stuffing herself with finka and coffee, though she left some uneaten. She was not usually the one to let food go to waste. Quite insane she had looked.

I had gone home almost straightaway. There was no understanding what she really thought.

The shit-house was at the top end, jammed in alongside the road.

If one opened the door to the shit-house – by the way, there were no shit-house cloths, only the *Norrie* – and sat down without closing it, one could see all the way out over the valley, over the lake and towards the marsh and even Ryss Island.

It was a little bit like being suspended over the valley. In the summer, it was good sitting there quite still hour after hour, looking out over the mirrorblank water of the lake. It used to be utterly silent, except for the cows.

I often thought of going there, even after the exchange, but since Mum, I mean Josefina, had come rushing out,

45

and looked dementit and left the finka uneaten so that maybe it would go to waste, I felt it was unnecessary.

I remember it was good in the shit-house and very silent, except the cows. This is how the shit-house was. Though this is perhaps not all that could be said. In *Nautilus*, there were other reminders of how it was.

He had not even tried to hide it. And what he wrote about was of course quite normal, nothing special at all, and there was no need to argufy about it.

I am just mentioning this, will come back to it later.

V

Concerning the cellar in the green house. Johannes's notes, from Captain Nemo's library.

In the cellar there were three rooms. One had an earth floor and was used as a potato store. It was dark, so that the potato-shoots should not grow: potatoes are like that, the greater darkness, the smaller growth. In the light, the shoots would grow, and the potatoes die. The idea was that in the dark, death would be kept at bay, though thinking about it, it was not a very good life for the potatoes if they were not allowed to die. The other room had an earth floor too, and was used as a larder, but there was no explanation of this thing about being dark.

In the third cellar-room in the green house there was a well in the floor where the water had very high iron content, and could not be used. There was real water only in the cold spring below the wild-rose hedge. That is, counting from the gable-end where the fire-escape ladder was, there was first the rowan tree, then the wild-rose hedge, then the slope down to the cold spring.

There were frogs in the cold spring. The water was very clean and pure, quite unlike the water in the cellar well. The water in the cold spring came from inside the mountain. The cold spring was only half a metre deep, and there were about ten frogs which had to be defended. All this about the potatoes was hard to fit together, but it seemed certain that whereas the dark made the potatoes edible, the light caused death, except if one planted the potatoes, then it made them alive. In this way the potatoes in the earth cellar were utterly confusing, and it was no good thinking too much about it, it was quite unnecessary.

But the frogs must be defended, no argufying about that.

In a way one was made a kind of keeper of animals, because not everyone knew how to defend the frogs. Bending over with the watterpail, to pail up fresh water from the cold spring, it was a matter of moving the pail sideways, somehow to steer it so that no frogs got into it and were pailed out to meet an uncertain future.

Of course the frogs cleaned the water, the well water in the earth cellar was sour, and the potatoes without shoots which would stay alive but were not allowed to die to rise again in this life on earth, put it that way, though anyway they probably were not frogs but toads. They were quite large and they said nothing special to note. The tadpoles were rather nice. One could keep tadpoles in the jam jars, without the lids. A tadpole, which often still had its tail on, wriggled in a special way when held in your hand. Josefina Marklund, my one-time mother, did not understand that the frogs must be defended.

On many occasions she pailed them out, so that they faced an uncertain future. It was difficult to be sure then if they lived or died. Protesting helped little, or not at all, still I believe that the frogs could find their way back. Not certain how.

But surely they felt homesick. Pailed out or not, homesickness does not disappear so easily.

I know that Josefina, my mother, even denied in front of other people from the village that we had frogs in the cold spring. This in spite of the known fact that frogs keep the water clean. It is important that it should be clean. Cleanliness was of course important. The water was clear. It was a matter of defending the frogs against those who knew no better. Those who thought frogs ugly or useless or repulsive surely did not understand that even the slimiest, and this accords with the Letter to the Corinthians, could be useful, yes, even more useful.

This is how I might be said to have become a kind of keeper of animals.

In the first cellar-space in the green house, the one with the potatoes, a trunk was kept for a long time. One day – 24 April, actually – one of my aunts came to collect this trunk. There is nothing more to add about the three cellar-rooms in the green house.

She had come to call, came with the bus one day and left the same evening. She was said to be an aunt.

She was tall and slim and had been striding out. A little

talk together had been performed between her and Josefina. She had not listened very carefully, but had realized that the two of them did not have much to talk about.

The aunt came from down south and was quite kind-eyed but elongated. She had apparently enquired a bit into the precise circumstances of the events involving the 'boys', as she put it in her southern speech, and got her answers. Not that Josefina had been hostile, or anything. The only thing the aunt had been clearly told was that it was unnecessary to discuss the matter in my case.

I was well enough off at Sven Hedman's. Nothing much to argufy about.

The aunt, who I was to see myself briefly down by the bus, was rather thin and elongated and came up to me by the bus, before it arrived, and asked if it was me. And I neither could nor would deny that. So she had bent down and embraced me quite without cause. And after she had been standing there for a very short while – perhaps it was more accurate to say that she gave me a 'hug' – I had torn myself away. Not for any special reason. But of course I did not want to be seen in that kind of situation, so I tore myself away.

That is how it was when I saw the aunt briefly down by the bus, which had come in from Forsen, that is from the Burträsk direction.

The trunk was another affair. But it concerned Johannes more than me.

The business with the trunk in the tattie-cellar was that she once had left it there when she travelled down south.

Something had happened. Hard to say what. And then she had travelled down south. But before she went away she had arrived with the trunk – from Boliden, I think – and had wanted to put it into the tattie-cellar. And Josefina had nothing to say to that. Then she left. And returned, actually on 24 April.

She was a bit thinner then and still very elongated. If I remember rightly from that short encounter by the bus, she had ugly shoes but quite kind eyes.

I cannot think what came over her, that she dared to bend down over me.

In the cellar, by the trunk, nothing special had happened.

Johannes remembered it quite well, he writes, that nothing special had happened.

She had gone down into the tattie-cellar. Her trunk was kept next to the potatoes, which were not to be chitted. It was more like a chest. She who was the aunt had gone down and Johannes had followed her. So she had found her way to the tattie-room. Then Johannes had turned on the light-bulb which hung right above. There was the trunk, which was more like a chest. And the aunt had taken out a key and turned it in the lock and opened it up.

And then she had stood there quietly for a while, looking into the trunk.

He had asked what there was. She had not answered. Then he leaned forward and looked. It seemed to be fabric, something like that, maybe a dress, maybe lace. It was hard to see.

She had stood there, looking. She was tall but bonnie, or at least that is how she was down by the bus when she left. Ugly shoes she wore, but had kind eyes. She was probably over forty. The trunk had been standing there for many years, but no one in the village had seen anything of her for a long time. They had just established, with some certainty, that she was an unmarried aunt, quite old, though younger than Josefina, who seemed not to like her very much, though that was neither here nor there, she had said.

And then the aunt had noticed a letter right up on top. It must have been for her, because she took the letter, opened it and read it silently. Afterwards she read the letter again. But then she snorted, upset somehow, and said: And that is what he says!!! and made a ball of the letter.

That was all. That was all he found out. It made him feel a bit let down.

She left the same evening. Eeva-Lisa helped her to carry the trunk down to the bus.

That was where I met her. And then she hugged me with Eeva-Lisa watching.

And then the bus left.

There was a kind of covered milk table as well. The trunk was a kind of chest, the milk table was a kind of house, the aunt had snorted and said so that is what he says. Many things were a kind of, or something like.

Eeva-Lisa had walked up from the road down there, when she came, up towards the green house.

The aunt had snorted.

I feel all empty now.

So that is how it was when Eeva-Lisa came.

But still, it must have started earlier.

I never found out why the aunt snorted like that.

It was something, I suppose.

I ought to have looked more closely at everyone with kind eyes to understand why they snort.

Tonight, a snowstorm.

2

AN INEXPLICABLE
MISTAKE

Eeva-Lisa was outside, deep in the snow,
   driven by pains and with nowhere to go.
The cold moon shone on the shit-house door,
   open and banging in the snow-wind's roar.

It hurt so much. She shut the door.
Dense thick dark and snow on the floor.
She sat there alone. Everyone sleeps —
   cannot see my shame — and only God weeps.

I

He scatters little notes with cheerful messages. In the larder in *Nautilus* under the butter-box, half-emptied after the finka fry-up, there is a note. 'The frogs must be defended.'

Obvious. He flatters himself with something I taught him.

However, there was no need to hide it under the butter-box.

Having things taken away makes one feel rather let down.

First they took my Mum away, then the horse, then Eeva-Lisa, then the deadboy, then the green house.

Who would have thought it can hurt so much to have a small house taken away. Though it was well built and ours, of course. It is natural for us to think that something is ours, that almost everything belongs to us, really. And then it turns out to be wrong. Lets one down, a bit. Quite flattening.

Still, there was no need for him to punish the house just because of that.

I myself felt let down all the time when I was growing up. Believed that at least the house could be saved if one drew it, carefully, using a lead pencil, I mean a timberman's pencil, like Dad did. Then I could take the drawing with me.

Salvage lists, that is what Dad called the poem in the notebook. It was his idea. That way quite a lot can be saved if one is in a great emergency in the cave of the dead cats.

My first thought, as I found him again on the kitchen sofa in *Nautilus* with the finka half-eaten and a roomful of texts and notes, was that he looked bonnie.

It is as if certain words from the house have stuck. Bonnie and dementit and let down and nocht.

Earlier I used to think that verses in hymns were useless because one had to learn them by heart and repeat them ceaselessly. Later I thought it made me feel safe in a way, to repeat and not have to think.

When I wake early in the morning and it is misty and the birds are asleep then I am happier if I keep repeating.

Bonnie. I have always wondered if I really wanted to be

bonnie, or just a traitor, like him. The focus of pain in a hymn-verse could perhaps be bonnie, and then the other words, which did not hurt, could be allowed to come too, in the other verses.

II

I met Johannes Hedman, as he was then called, for the first time when he was about two years old and staying with the Hedmans. Later, we played with each other all the time up to the exchange. Then there was a break when Eeva-Lisa had come to make him feel less nervous. Afterwards it seemed that we played more at a distance.

And then all that happened.

In between there was the exchange. I shall tell that story first, and then it is done. One must get it over and done with, it is not the worst bit, and then it is done.

Very few believed the story at first. Then everybody believed it, except the Hedmans.

Really, the Hedmans were to be pitied most. First they had Johannes, who was so bonnie, then just me, then Alfhild Hedman became a horse and in the end Sven Hedman surely had next to nothing left. I think he was completely at a loss about what to do.

It is dreadful, being completely at a loss. I suppose that is why he visited me when I stayed silent and patted me on the muzzle as if I had been a horse. But maybe he realized that I was no longer sure of being properly human any more.

Though what is wrong with animals.

I believe that in fact everybody got frightened of Sven

and Alfhild and me because we were not quite sure of being human. And if one is not certain in oneself, how can other people be sure. The first time I felt almost human, after the exchange, was when the elongated aunt hugged me down by the bus, in spite of Eeva-Lisa watching. That was the only hug I got in my entire life. If one really thinks about it. Though it was close that time I was speaking to Eeva-Lisa about those tulips growing downwards.

Bus-stop, hug, elongated aunt; and that is meant to be one of life's high points. Unbelievable.

Still that is how it was.

It began one day in January 1939, when it was so cold the pissbucket on the first floor, the one standing at the top of the inside stairs, had frozen to yellow ice. Though it was inside the house. Josefina had complained that things were at a pretty pass when one had to use the poker on the pissbucket, and might as well make heat to warm the crows, because they surely did not enjoy themselves either. She even got tender-hearted about the crows when the piss froze in the bucket, that was some kind of measure of how cold it was.

I remember it well. I was four years old and had to go and dump the block of piss into the snow. It was Sunday morning. No preacher was coming, the inflatable tyres on the bicycle must have frozen, so James (pronounced Schamese) Lindgren was to read from Rosenius. Mum took the knitted muff, although we were just going across the yard.

I wore fleecyboots. The block of piss gleamed yellow in the snow. I was not particularly cheerful, no one was when

James Lindgren was due to read from Rosenius, but it would probably only last some two hours, because the chapel was cold. However it was a matter of being tough.

I did not know then that this reading would change my life.

Sven Hedman's wife was called Alfhild, and was said to come from a family of tinkers. They could also have been Walloon, from over Hörnefors way, but the general opinion was tinker. Everybody knew that tinkers were light-fingered, so it was no joke for Sven Hedman who had brought the woman along, however at the time she was still beautiful.

She was to be pitied too. She could not speak properly, but that was not due to her being a tinker, possibly, or perhaps a Walloon. General opinion held that she became half mute when she got Johannes. That is how it was his fault, and it was felt that I could well be blamed later, after the exchange.

The muteness struck her in the cottage hospital. Until then she had been chatting away like everybody else, and she had a beautiful singing voice, clearly audible in the yellow chapel. If she had not been a tinker everyone would probably have liked her. Now people stayed somehow watchful, just generally.

After the birth in September 1934 the muteness struck her, though not the singing voice. God's words came out of her completely clear and precise when she was singing the hymns. It was like a miracle. It must have been a comfort to her. If only she had not become my mother later on, I would probably have liked her, I think.

She returned home from Bureå cottage hospital with a child, whom she christened Johannes. However quite soon

57

it was whispered that there was something not right about the child she had christened Johannes. Unlike hers, the child's appearance was not that of a tinker. It looked practically bonnie, with blue eyes and blond hair, regular features and shapely teeth. His smile was bright and open, his laugh came easily, and it did not take long before he was everyone's favourite.

It was established in a general way that there was something odd about his appearance, taking hers into account. Nor did he look like Sven Hedman. But because nobody wanted to contest that Alfhild was the mother of the child, after a while it got to be quite unnecessary to dwell on this. So it was probably the Son of Man sent back to the world once more, said Egon Fahlman from Östra Hjoggböle, who was no believer but a shoemaker, it was a joke, no one thought it proper, but they said that he had said it.

We lived five hundred metres from the Hedmans, across the valley. The odd thing was, I looked a bit like Alfhild Hedman. That was the start of it all. That is how it was that day in January 1939 when the pissbucket froze, the preacher did not come, James Lindgren was to read Rosenius and my life was to change.

Otherwise, there were no tinkers in the village, thank the Lord.

However, there was a tinkers' place in Forsen, which was between Sjön and Östra Hjoggböle. That is where the Co-op was, it was really called Koppra, and the tinkers' place was there. The tinkers' place was a house, over in the Skellefte direction, on Kleppen. Every now and then tinkers from Finland turned up there too.

When they came they wanted to do tinning. It was almost

worse than when a Jehovah's Witness stopped by on a Good Friday. No one had anything to be tinned, until the day when there had been a night-time fire on a farm, where the tinkers had been briskly refused.

After that practically everybody wanted tinning done. It was of course almost certain there was a connection, even if all the places where there had been a firm and decisive *no* did not go on fire.

There was something odd about Alfhild, Eeva-Lisa and the tinkers. In the library Captain Nemo made a note of it.

But all the same. Anyway, it does not concern Johannes, who was fair-skinned, had a bright smile and was well liked by everyone.

Apparently, he has done research.

Eeva-Lisa's grandfather was, by her own account, although there were no gypsies in the family, an expert on gypsy life and had compiled a dictionary of the gypsies' secret vocabulary. When questioned about this language she would become quite silent. Since the purpose of the language was to protect the gypsies from a threatening society, it was vital to maintain the secrecy. For five years he had travelled about in southern Finland, among Finnish gypsies, and assisted by a young Hungarian boy, allegedly called Palo, had recorded the secrets.

When it all came out in published form it was revealed that he had been hoodwinked. Everything which he had recorded, words, syntax, the whole card-index of secrets, was a deception. He believed himself to be the explorer, but the boy had wanted to protect himself, and so he had invented a language for his own defence. Palo had spun him a tale, to save himself. When this became known her grandfather fled to northern Argentina, to Misiones, because the shame became unbearable. There, her mother had died in strange circumstances, while her grandfather had concealed himself in a smaller community called Guarany, close to the Brazilian border.

However, the records of the secret language have been preserved by the boy, Palo, who had in fact created it himself on false premises.

I do not know how she came to us.

Afterwards I thought that of course there are many who are not quite human humans, and who could have got together.

No secret language would be needed for this. Or maybe one would need a secret language.

But no, but no.

In a certain species of albatross, birds bigger and more powerful than Eeva-Lisa and I, there exists a phenomenon called the 'Cain syndrome'. The bird hatches two, occasionally as many as three, eggs. The bird sits on the eggs as they are laid. In this way the eggs are hatched with a few days between them. Then the older baby albatross pecks the younger one to death. Nobody knows why.

It has got food. Love too.

I am a strange and unusual baby in that case. He pecked me to death six years after I was born, in spite of us having been born at the same time.

So it is not to be wondered at, that I took the life of my murderer.

III

It was very cold that Sunday, but the mid-current in the burn was still free of ice, as always. The smell of rotten eggs reached far away. It must have been thirty-five degrees under.

A low sun, now at midday it was just two fingers' breadths above the horizon.

Mum wore the knitted muff. Sat there wearing it in the chapel too. Everybody kept their outdoor clothes on. The vapour from their mouths made it hard to see the Saviour in the picture.

In front of us Alfhild Hedman was sitting, with Johannes.

At the far end of the chapel, next to the stove, it was very hot. Further forward it was cool, then freezing cold. The painting showed the Son of Man reaching out with his hands over the poor children, and the frame of the picture had a chip out of it. 'Jesus loves the little children' the revivalist song was called; later Johannes set his lying verses about Eeva-Lisa to its tune.

Aunt Hanna was sitting on the other side of the central aisle. She was watching us intently all the time.

After two hours it was over, because it was so cold that James Lindgren could scarce keep life in his feet and started stomping so it became hard to follow.

Everybody went home, Aunt Hanna too. Later we heard how it went. She had gone home and been very silent. All night she had stayed awake, praying for guidance. The following day she got on to the telephone to other firm believers, who also knew a thing or two about what had happened. Finally also Mum, who then got together with Aunt Hanna and talked for a long time.

So in the end Josefina had come out from the bedroom where they had been sitting so as to cause no one any trouble. And she looked quite woebegone, but said nothing to me, who was wondering after all.

She must have been made to tell what happened that time in the cottage hospital. And then presumably Aunt Hanna had got her worst suspicions confirmed. And so began the great misfortune.

The cottage hospital in Bureå was in a quite pretty situation.

The great river ran only a hundred metres down, through a birchwood. But one could see the river. The patients' rooms all had windows facing south.

As it happened, Josefina and Alfhild Hedman came to give birth the same day. One was five hours or so ahead, they said. And they were in the same ward.

It was a fine autumn, the leaves were yellow and stayed put and no snow had fallen on them. And the following morning, Mrs Stenberg, the midwife, had entered ward number two in the cottage hospital carrying two babies in her arms. Both boys. And had been a bit harassed but cheerful enough. And so she had said in her humorous slightly cross way, which could occasionally be misunderstood, that now it was time for food.

And whose baby was this anyway.

They later said about her that this had been the ruin of her life and that she went to her grave ruined and was never quite herself again and many other unhappy things were said. She was remembered chiefly for her unhappiness. But at the time she had mostly been humorous. Afterwards, as the case started spreading throughout Sweden, first in little circles in the parish, then in wider and wider circles, until like a mighty wave it rolled on even down to Stockholm and the people who read the papers there, everybody asked how it could possibly have happened. 'This was the question on everyone's mind,' it said.

But since that time, there has been just one question on my mind. Not how it happened, if it happened. But if I was truly human.

And, if so: who.

The latterly not-so-well-liked midwife entered and asked which child belonged to whom.

And Alfhild Hedman, who at the time usually pointed, because something inexplicable seemed to have happened to her voice, she pointed. And it was only natural to recognize one's own child. And so she was handed Johannes.

And that is how things stood, until the dizzying moment when suddenly Aunt Hanna, when she like everyone else in the chapel was not listening to Rosenius, and clouds of vapour were coming out of her mouth, and watched by the friend of little children in the picture with a chip out of its frame, had stared at the two boys and asked herself if there had not been a switch after all.

And the next day she herself had raised the question.

And so it began.

Why was it necessary. Surely it could have been all right as it was.

There is nothing strange about exchanges, they told me afterwards.

There are of course many well-known changelings. Mowgli, for instance, in *The Jungle Book*. Almost always the stories were nice, and the point was a nice little person, a king's child really, had been carelessly lost. Or had lived among wolves. If one lived among animals perhaps one got the same feelings and thoughts as them but in the end it was still all right. One got back to the house at last. To the king's house sometimes.

There had been a very bad time, but then there was a homecoming, like the prodigal son. And there was much joy.

But of course I had to leave the green house.

I have hated really only one person in my whole life. And her I hardly knew. It was Aunt Hanna.

Why then was all this necessary. They stole my Mum from me, and my Dad's house, and the summerbothy, and the shit-house and the cold spring and the frogs and the rowan, which was a lucky tree.

Being switched means that one is never quite sure if one is a real human being. Not like before, anyway. I realized too late that I had to die and rise again and seek out the company of those not quite truly human, perhaps horses, perhaps the cats under the varnish on the bed-end.

Aunt Hanna apparently never doubted that she was human. But she stared intently at us in chapel, and then she turned me into somebody else.

I wish Eeva-Lisa had been there that day in the chapel. Oh, I wish it so much.

She could have made a sign to the friend of little children

in the picture. Or, if he was pressed for time, called on Captain Nemo, who was a benefactor to all those in dire need.

But nocht.

IV

It amounted to a lot of parleys. I call it that.

Links were forged, as in Granddad's smithy. There was Aunt Hanna, and then Josefina and then the vicar, whose wife had a suitcase, and the doctor, who looked into the paperwork, and the midwife, who could absolutely not recall it. Then the police, and the local correspondent from the *Norrie*. He was paid per line. And so the links were forged.

The worst thing was to see it in the paper, but without names. Then I knew straightaway.

I became good at knowing if it was me who was mentioned, though without a name. There is a certain something in the air when it is oneself.

If I had known that Sunday maybe I could have crawled into the lap of the Son of Man. Through the varnish covering the picture. He who is said to help all the children. But now I was sitting there instead next to Mum, who was wearing the knitted muff. Cannot remember anything. So I could just as soon imagine that she stroked my hair a little with her hand, a bit absently, as if she was deep in Rosenius but still thoughtfully stroked my hair. Just a little, lightly.

What is there to lose by imagining. Though she was not one to stroke hair unnecessarily. To be tickled like a cat. Just at that moment Aunt Hanna decided to take justice into her own hands, the forging of the chain began, the sledgehammer was raised over the link, the iron burnt, and I was on my way to losing my life.

It was a sensation which was going to be widely known, I realized later.

The circles spread on the water. Inside the innermost circle, that around Johannes and me and Mum and Alfhild, all was calm and shining and still. At first. But then the wave roared everywhere. In all the newspapers, and the radio, and in the Stockholm press, where much was made of the changeling affair in the tiny distant village in Norrland. That is to say us. Just because they were far away we were distant. But we were right in the centre of it. They were the distant ones.

Actually, it is dreadful to be in the centre. I would like to be distant.

It was the vicar, who had me in for a special parley, at the mothers' request, and he told me.

He told the story, after praying briefly, I have forgotten what the prayer was about, of how we had been switched in the maternity ward. There had quite simply been a mix-up. It was not hopeless, though, since justice must be done, it was just a matter of what the courts had to say and Swedish justice was immutable. I thought he said immootable and thought it sounded like something to do with cows. We had got the wrong mothers. Now we were going to get the right mothers. He did not mention the house, and I did not ask and cried not at all, for which he praised me heartily and then said a prayer to round it off.

If it at least had been preacher Forsberg, who had a

bicycle with inflatable tyres and seven children and was used to it.

It was to take its time. But time heals all wounds. I was going to get my proper mother, that meant Alfhild Hedman, and Johannes was to get his rightful one, that meant Josefina.

Sven Hedman was not mentioned. They are said to have refused. That is why at last it went to the Supreme Court. Presumably there had been nothing like it before.

But it was not what I was going to get, what was to become my share, that was burnt into me. It was not about Alfhild and Sven Hedman. It was what I lost that was burning. I was going to lose the green house and the summerbothy, which looked like a boat house, and the woodshed and the shit-house with copies of the *Norrie*. And the wild-rose hedge and the rowan, which in the winter had snow and berries and birds. And the cold spring with the frogs, which I would no longer be able to defend.

Before the prayer to round it off, the vicar asked me if I had any questions. I said no. For this too I was heartily praised.

Mum was not in when the vicar called.

I do not know what they said to Johannes of course.

Perhaps they said the same things. Perhaps for him too, the important thing was what he lost, not what he was about to get.

We never talked about it, though. Not a single word did we exchange about it. And when after a break of a couple of years we started playing with each other again he had of course been given Eeva-Lisa, so he would not be nervous.

Which is why I do not know what my best friend Johannes thought about it all, the most important thing to happen to him, apart from the betrayal and what happened on the stairs, when Eeva-Lisa was taken away from him.

But then he got the green house.

Truly, he got it from me. It was taken from me and given to him. And I was handed over with nothing. Quite empty, like snails, a little slime, a bit of shell, rather dead, nothing much really. If one has owned something, and it is taken away, then one knows what is lost. If one has never had anything, then surely it cannot be so dreadful to lose nothing.

Just before it all happened, and before Aunt Hanna had fixed us with the evileye that day in chapel and started to parley with the Saviour, I had got a cat. But Josefina sent it away, because it shat on the iron range. She thought it quite unnecessary what the wee cat did. It was the only cat I have had. I had it at first, and then I did not have it. Better if I had never had a cat, then surely it would not have been so dreadful. Better never to have had, better never to have had, then one does not become dementit, almost, when it is taken away.

What I mean is: we left the chapel that day, Johannes and I, quite cheerful because the reading from Rosenius had ended. One became quite happy each Sunday when it came to an end. Somehow it brightened up all the Sundays, that moment of getting out.

But if one had not had to suffer Rosenius, read by James (pronounced Schamese) Lindgren, then of course one would not have been so happy at the end. It must be the same thing, but the other way round, with the green house.

We got out, the sun had set, because it was already past one o'clock and it was January.

I stood on the chapel porch, and in a way I had reached the centrepoint of my life. And yet I was only four and a half years old.

Once I had a dog as well, but just for a day, then they found the owner.

I am certain the cat could have learnt not to shit on the iron range. There is something sick about people who take away what one has got.

I must steel myself. One must steel oneself, always. Now I shall tell the story of how we were switched back.

V

The Supreme Court found, with great probability, bordering on certainty, Alfhild Hedman to be my mother.

Johannes was not carted off by the police. He took it all as if it were quite natural, I think, but never asked.

Josefina declared, supported by Aunt Hanna with the evileye, that justice must take its course. Surely, there was something in the blackbible about it. If one wanted to search, all evil could probably be found in there. She wanted to switch back again, and she was supported by Aunt Hanna. The Hedmans did not believe in the Supreme Court, but what could they do.

I really did not look much like a tinker either. More like Sven Hedman as it happens. They kept investigating our ears. Something to do with the convolutions. As if on a shell. Not human, really.

The decision was announced in the *Norrie*.

After the Sheriff had left, having handed over the papers, which Mum did not bother to read although it was a victory, I started going over the house in order to be able to construct more exactly a ground-plan with an inventory of the position of things.

We had a kind of white paper on a roll in the larder. When Mum had gone out to parley with Aunt Hanna, I pulled the paper out and tore off a metre-long piece. Then I got out an ordinary lead pencil, it was a timberman's pencil, which Mum had saved from Dad, I call them so. He had used it in the timber forest while he was felling and heaving about. I think he wrote in his notebook with it.

I began, on the paper, using the timberman's pencil, to set out the detailed inventory of the house.

I had to take care. I must not make a single mistake. Then, somehow, the green house would be lost for ever. It was like the salvage lists from the stranded ship in *Robinson Crusoe*.

Time pressed, because the vicar had been most serious on the phone.

Mum did not say much these days. But I was probably not worth talking to much.

I carefully drew the whole house.

The cellars, the tattie-cellar where chitting was not allowed, the earth cellar, and the room with the well with the bad water, worse than the cold spring with the frogs, the cellars were the easiest. I could draw that quite calmly, almost indifferently, like another Batman. The stairs down were easily drawn too.

I say this quite honestly.

Upstairs had to be exact. I measured the size of the rooms in feet, and used Dad's old inch-rule. One might ask what Dad would have said about it all, one might well ask. The iron range I drew with all its details, cooking rings, oven, and urn. The log box, where I used to sit while Mum was cooking and just look, thinking of nothing special, or thinking of the war, if Mum was talking about something exciting she had read in the paper, the box I drew roughly, with the logs only hinted at.

It was getting to look quite good, and I was only six.

It got harder by the first floor. That was the worst part of the salvage list.

VI

She found me up in the attic just when I had brought the whole salvage list to a close.

I had drawn in the bedroom and managed quite well. I had used a lath as a ruler. The bedroom looked good: measurements fine, the window in the right place. My little pull-out bed, where I slept, had taken quite some time.

In the drawing, one thing could not be put in properly, the most important part, that is to say the inside of the head-end of the bed. The old varnish on it, so old it could have been Granddad, if Granddad is the right word to say, who applied it, the varnish had quite gradually bubbled, darkened and discoloured in strips, so that figures, trees and forests began to emerge without the bed-end being able to do anything to cover it up. When Granddad first varnished it over, it had surely stayed normal for quite a long time. But finally the figures and the trees had emerged.

It was best in the summer. Then it was light all night long, and I could either not go to sleep or decide to wake up. Mum would be asleep then, I mean Josefina Marklund, and snoring, but that did not matter.

I would sit by the bed-end and look at the animals. They were all brown and looked sort of kind. They were cats, mostly, one could see their ears clearly, and the eyes on some of them; but also birds, with the outlines of their wings cutting across the sky above the brown animals.

Sometimes it was hard to be sure what kind of animals they were. Some of them seemed troubled, or unhappy, there were three or four which caused me serious worry because of their sad faces, their tears kept back only with an effort. One baby animal seemed pale and perhaps it was dying, as if the father had been a drunkard, but by and large one could not be sure what had happened.

One had to imagine. It was easy to see the mouths on many of the cats, they often moved, especially on some very light summer nights. They sort of asked for advice. I got the notion they were all greatly perplexed. Exactly what they were speaking about of course I did not know, but the movements of their mouths and eyes were full of needs to satisfy and one in particular (perhaps it was a dog) was utterly perplexed.

The landscape itself was the way one would imagine it.

In the winter, the animals must still have been there, but one could not see them. It had to be enough to feel them with one's hands.

I know that all these animals, which had pushed their way through the varnish, enclosed me in their great concern. I did too, towards them. I was quite desperate to think that they were to be left lonesome, and without a benefactor or adviser to help them in their perplexity.

Johannes, who was to take over this bed, and this bed-end with the worried and puzzled animals, was sure not to understand. One does not, if one is bonnie and well liked by everyone. To understand, and understand rightly, the moving mouths of the varnish-animals, one must be otherwise.

I drew the bed-end. But not the animals.

Once Mum had said that I was to get the sandpaper and then she would put on more varnish, because it looked recht peteous.

I almost died. Luckily she forgot.

I drew Mum's bed as well. Likewise the bedside table with the basin and ewer with water, and the bowl with green soap and the towels. I drew the glass with the salt water too.

Besides, there were just two wooden chairs and the box in which I kept two books.

The Bible was on the bedside table. The *Bible for Children* was kept in the box too. It was not as enjoyable as the large family Bible downstairs. That one had the pictures, including the one with the Flood and the women with practically no clothes on, who were being engulfed.

It was quite horrible to see how they looked, but beautiful in a way. They were engulfed by the great flood waters and so had not the sense to cover themselves. An enormous hole had formed in the great flood waters, as if it was the hole in the side of the Son of Man, where one could crawl in and hide. They were sucked into it, all these bare women in the picture from the big Bible.

Everything could be drawn in. I drew without pain. The attic came last.

What was I going to put in.

The unused bed in the corner. The planks. The wall that had not been painted and had no old varnish on it and was entirely without animals. The game-board with holes Dad had made, the Korong-board. The hole-board was like a chess-board but one used cardboard counters with crosses on the back; surely he could have played a few games on it, even though it would perhaps have been sinful. Perhaps. I would have known that, if he had been alive and if he had been my father (but the Supreme Court). The bread peels, large, a metre wide and very thin with the initials burnt in with the branding iron. One might ask why he had wanted the fiddle. Anyway, where was the fiddle. Had she burnt that too. Everything was burnt but then it was just as well to burn everything. The cubby-hole with the papers which were dreadfully old. The rolling-pin.

There was so much. I did not have time. Time was so short. The hole-board. Was there a fiddle and why had he bought it and why did they keep so quiet about him. I mean, I must have come from somewhere. Surely it was not the Holy Spirit.

The rolling-pin. The hole-board.

And then I gave up.

I had been lying down on the pile of newspapers in the attic cubby-hole and had started crying when Josefina came.

First she asked what was the matter. Then she did not bother to ask any more, though I kept on greeting. The ground-plan on the kitchen paper, it was more like grease-proof paper, was on the floor and she looked to see if it had been drawn properly.

Mum was not one to pat or stroke someone unnecessarily.

She was really beautiful, I had always thought that. But there is no need to be beautiful. And when Dad died, that is to say when Johannes's Dad died, it was as if she had become mute. She was just as beautiful as before, everyone said so, but she was silent. That is how I came from one mother, who was beautiful, but silent, to another, that was Alfhild, who was not as beautiful but silent too, in another way.

Because she was silent, Josefina did not like to pat. Or to be patted. All that was quite unnecessary, I came to know that.

Maybe that is why I got so frightened that time when the rather elongated aunt hugged me down by the bus.

She sat down next to the pile of newspapers and somehow did not moan aloud.

I wonder how old she was then.

She did not say anything. What could she say. It was decided, it had been decided.

Though for more than six years, she had had me.

After she had been sitting there for quite a long time somehow not moaning aloud, and I had stopped greeting and it was so silent that not even the aspens outside could be heard, she got up from the pile of newspapers where I was lying. She had said nothing at all. She crossed the attic floor, to the sugar-loaf in the corner. She then took the sugar-tongs and cut it. She took the piece in her hand, carefully put the sugar-tongs down again, and came back to me.

I wonder how old she was. I always thought she was so beautiful.

She took the cut sugar-lump and licked it a little to soften it. Then she held the cut-sugar very close to my mouth.

I did not know what to do. I waited.

She held the sugar-lump close to my mouth. I had stopped greeting. It was quite silent in the attic.

She did not take her hand away, she just waited. I shall always remember that. I remember how she looked. And at last I understood what to do: I parted my lips and with the very tip of my tongue I touched the white harsh surface of the sugar.

They brought me across with the help of the Sheriff.

I have seen the picture. It was in the paper.

It is snowing, the picture is blurred, perhaps by snow on the lens of the camera. The picture is blurred, but one can see everything anyway, how they are carrying me and how I am screaming desperately, enclosed in the Sheriff's arms.

VII

Why should I blame him for the fire. Anyway, I do not, not any more.

I suppose he could not make it fit together, or did not

76

try to. He must have been immured in the library of the submarine for too long. That would make one dementit, I suppose.

I shall never tell about how he tried to punish the green house.

The executioners, the victims and the traitors.
Signal.
There is ticking from the outermost edges of space, from him to me, secret messages about a life. 'Signals from the dead stars' was the kind of thing he wrote when he was really explicit. 'I believe that is when I died', that is about her who was taken away from him.
A striking fixation on death inside someone who is alive.

He had escaped from the hospital, travelled all the way and tried to burn the house down and himself in it. But it had not worked as well as he had hoped.

I went over to stand at the bedroom window and looked out over the valley. It was as it should be, snow and the moonlight all white. There was smoke. I had imagined it differently, it should burn without hurting, embedded in snow like wadding, and with the whining of the telephone wires in the cold, a song coming from the outermost edges of space, and the rowan with snow and birds in front of me. But there was no song, only smoke coming in, and I was saved although I did not want to be and fought it. Nothing became how I wanted it.

It was as if I could not remember anything right. The slope down to the cold spring was completely flat, there were no frogs to be saved, the attic with the *Norries* was emptied. The house could not be punished, nor made to stop living, when it did not want to. If one does not deserve death then one is denied it. And so must carry on. One must not try to deserve mercy either. But perhaps one must try to deserve death, or it would not be living. There will always be something better on offer than death, said the donkey. Come on, Redcomb, let us carry on. That was why they came to save me.

No storm any more.

When there was a storm the gulls flew slowly past my window, driven back by the wind, looking at me with their melancholic little smiles, whispering almost soundlessly.

Do you remember us, they said. From the bed-end with the varnish. We are still trying, we have not given up. Then they were swept backwards by the storm, still flying.

Now the sea breathes.

Staying this summer and winter near to the sea, at the southernmost border of Sweden. As far as possible away from what happened, but within the border. To sum it up.

So I am adding things up, within, but at the border.

Woke tonight with a high fever, and dreamt pain. My whole body shook, but calmed down after a few minutes. It was like that time, before the exchange, those times I ran a temperature. I was sweating at night and called for Josefina. She came padding through the darkness, her voice almost wheedling, because it was so dark that there was no need for her to feel ashamed about it.

The sheets were wet from the fever. So she lit the lamp, changed the sheets and my longjohns, which had got wet too, and my under-shirt. All was dry then and she put out the lamp. Afterwards I was lying there completely calm and looking up into the ceiling where the snow-light shone like a white calm quiet fire. The animals in the forest in the bed-end slept, wrapped tightly in their dreams, like the birds on the water. And so I could sleep as well.

Perhaps death will be like this in the end: not the one which comes in life, but the last one. It will be like when Mum changes the sheets, and it feels dry and warm again, the birds sleep, the snow-light warms and I can sleep.

I have been fairly calm since I found him again in Captain Nemo's library. Not quite been myself, just because I have been calm.

Sleep on.

Towards the evening black rain came rolling in from the south, it came like a swiftly growing wall moving in over the ridge of hills along the coast and pressed down on the grass and whipped it and then quietly vanished upwards and to the north: it became utterly calm and clear.

I walked up on the ridge of hills. One could see Bornholm like a shadow far away in the south. The water was breathing in very slow movements, strangely black, almost like the water at the core of the Franklin volcano.

I walked for many hours that night. I found a kitten, lying there quite lifeless. There were plenty of wild cats round here. The kitten was perhaps a month old, no more. It was lying still in the grass, it snout pointing seawards, keeping its eyes closed. It was wet through.

I could feel the heart beating and beating.

I carried it down to the house. The kitten kept its eyes stubbornly closed, refused to open them though it must have been old enough. The cats in the bed-end slept just like this, but woke when I called them. Often, it was them calling to me. I miss them still.

Pus was seeping out from the eyes of the kitten. I tried to open its eyes and succeeded. The birds had got there ahead of me, the eyes were pecked away.

So.

I walked over the ridge down towards the beach.

Twilight had fallen, from beach-stones I built a last pit for the kitten, with a flat stone at the bottom. I placed the kitten on the flat stone at the bottom, this is how kittens are killed. I too had also learnt this about death: it was practical, without sentimentality, a swift painless ending.

Not that there is a choice. The swift death and the inner death did not know each other. They were both ignorant and innocent of each other. The kitten sat with its eyes firmly closed in the bottom of the pit.

I looked at the kitten. So many years have passed. It is so difficult to get it all to add up, and so necessary. I took a stone and let it drop on the kitten.

How old I had become since I fled from the green house. Over the big stone I put other stones. There was hardly a mound to be seen on the surface of the beach.

I walked westwards over the ridge to Ale's Stones. Early night hovered over the sea, Bornholm was out of sight. There were snails everywhere in the grass, I could hear them crunch under the soles of my shoes. Johannes did not want to stay with me and had never come back. That was not how it should be in the end. Crunching underfoot, and the twilight filled with an immense beauty and a completely normal death.

It began with the exchange.

I shall fit things together tonight. Josefina was so bonnie when she changed the sheets, but when I came back after the exchange she did not want to talk to me.

Signs.

Message: 'We must go far further.'

Signal.

How silent it is tonight.

Outside the birds are asleep. The animals in the bed-end still have not called me. Perhaps they do not need a benefactor, because they have still not found themselves in utter wretchedness.

II

THE AFFAIR OF THE HORSE

1

ALFHILD

God cares for little children
  even this whore-child is fine.
The church-folk ogled last Sunday
  at that big belly of mine.

Eeva-Lisa's legs are braced,
  warm coat and cold light of the moon.
Maybe from her womb the Saviour
  will be born in this shit-house room.

I

When the Sheriff had carried me into my new home I had
been given new fleecyboots, and there was a photographer
with him from the *Norrie* and another one from a Stockholm picture magazine, who had taken the train down
from Luleå just for this. The Sheriff had not carried me
all the way, just the first fifty metres down the slope. Then
I had walked on my own.

Sven Hedman received us in the kitchen on his own. Alfhild was at home, but had turned very silent and sung, to the melody of 'When Christmas Morning Light Gleams', that she did not want to show herself to the photographers.

Quarter of an hour later the three of us had been left alone. I was given rye-flour porridge on a flatplate with plenty of molasses. Only Sven Hedman and I ate. He pressed food on me a little with the kindvoice. It stands to reason that I did not like them.

He was probably scared and had cooked some food he knew he could manage. In the green house we never ate molasses, it was regarded as feed for the cows, which was not right, molasses was as good as syrup and cheaper. It was typical, Sven Hedman said long afterwards, that Josefina tried to make herself a bit grand about the molasses. To which I did not respond.

Generally he took care not to speak ill of her. The only time it came was about the molasses.

Stands to reason he was afraid.

The Supreme Court was the highest legal authority in the nation and had established that he, the former bullkeeper, had been in the wrong, and sentenced him to have me. It must be quite solemn to get a child through a sentence passed in the Supreme Court. He ought to feel a bit uncommon even, but just became silent. Alfhild was of course silent already, except when she sang. But then she probably did not have the sense.

Many surely thought it was almost too solemn a misfortune to be inflicted on insignificant smallholders. Somehow it did not befit the likes of them.

I am certain he much preferred Johannes, who was bonnie.

Previously, Sven Hedman had been the village bull-keeper, which was an honour, especially when taking into account that he had no cows; he cut timber during the winters and went on to the boats at Bure in the summers and was not really even a smallholder. After a few years the honorary task, that is of being bull-keeper, was taken away from him, and then he became taciturn.

He had married Alfhild because she was beautiful. She came from down south.

She was no longer beautiful. General opinion in the village held that she may have been beautiful at first, when he brought her along, but that she had dried up since then and was no longer beautiful. Ugly, if anything. There was something Lapp-like about her body, maybe not the body but the way she walked, and the face was not worth speaking about. Her hair was beautiful, but she was far too wrinkled.

Sven Hedman may well have had his own view once, but not any more. Perhaps he had got a piece of glass in his eye, so perhaps he saw her as ugly, or at least shrivelled up. Everybody else thought so. Why should he do otherwise. When she had her child, and the stroke at the same time, she became even uglier.

The most beautiful thing he knew must have been Johannes.

He had got me through a sentence in court. So he surely saw me that way too, through that piece of glass. I and Alfhild became something ugly. But he received me kindly when I was carried there, and prepared rye-flour porridge with plenty of molasses. He poured out the rye-flour porridge on a flatplate and made a well in the middle for the molasses and handed me a spoon, and then we ate from one side each. That was the family way, so to speak. He seemed to be trying to cheer me up, by not giving me a plate of my own, and I noticed that at the end he left the molasses-well for me. He must have been sorry that the precious bairn was gone and have steeled himself in spite of everything becoming so ugly.

When he came back home from the timber forest and saw us, Alfhild and me, in the kitchen, surely he just saw that we were ugly.

Because he was afraid of us I did not talk much with him. He was heavily built, quite bald, had never been much for the quaens, they said, and took snuff all the time. Lots of people were surprised, almost stunned, that time when he brought Alfhild along.

Of course there were those who remembered well how she looked when she came. It had been odd. But then it turned out not to be much to argufy about.

I had the kitchen sofa. They slept in the parlour.

There were no cats in the head-board of the kitchen sofa. I could not even look out at the rowan. There were neither birds nor snow in the rowan I could not see. All I could see was Alfhild and Sven Hedman. They did not speak to each other.

I can speculate, today, that they grieved. So why should they speak to each other. They got on anyway. What happens happens. Johannes was gone. Everything was like new shiny ice without sun. I was lying on the kitchen sofa. I too had become like shiny ice.

This is how Alfhild Hedman became a horse.

One year and three months after the exchange Alfhild Hedman had her second stroke.

She survived that one too. But she was not even like the way she had been before.

I wonder sometimes what people thought she would come to mean to me. A kind of mother, I suppose. Perhaps they thought that she would be sitting there in the black-dress with her blackhair, singing to me from the Songs of Zion; because she could sing of course. And she would sit there with her head in her hand and sing of God's love for the beloved child she had just got back.

But the only thing I really noticed, when I came that time, was her ugliness, and how silent it was. It was strange, but I seem to have forgotten how important it was to defend the frogs. I was so absorbed by how ugly and silent everything was, that I forgot what little I had learnt.

I think I tried to sleep as much as possible. But as much as I would have liked – that was impossible.

She had her second stroke on a Wednesday.

First she was taken to the cottage hospital where they had had the mix-up between Johannes and me; there she was left to look after herself. Then she came home, and so I had to look after her. They brought her one day towards the end of February; she came on the bus, was put into a buggy, we had no spare horse but she was so light I and Sven could pull her.

She was put on the kitchen sofa. We propped her up with cushions.

Then, for the time being, there were just her and Sven

and me. She was to become a horse later on. Though not until the summer.

Quite often she kept her eyes closed. Perhaps she too had a few brown varnish-cats to call to, with her eyes closed in her darkness.

If they did not call to her.

I have speculated, since, how it was between her and Sven Hedman.

There must have been some kind of love. Why else should he take up with someone who was like a tinker, and maybe was Walloon. He must have realized that this would be a source of much pain. He must have been afraid of loneliness, and there is no knowing what they talked about while she still could talk. She too might have been afraid. In the village, they said that in the early years Sven and Alfhild were like the beast of burden with two heads in the Book of Revelations. But maybe Sven and Alfhild did nct know that they lived in great pain. If one does not know of the pain it does not exist.

Therefore it must have been love. If one lives in pain but without realizing it, the cause must be love.

It was at the beginning of May that the deterioration set in. Sven wanted it to be kept within the family. That was surely the root of the problem.

At first the deterioration was so slight that we hardly noticed it. A bit like how it is when a great misfortune turns into a very great misfortune. She was not just mute, but thoughtful. We understood that something had happened.

Then came the next stage when she was thoughtful but not entirely mute. Then we began to get it.

The worst thing was her not being mute any more. She shat herself a bit too.

Sven Hedman managed most of it of course, but sometimes I helped. Sometimes when Sven was away in the forest it was I who ought to, but I fought a bit shy. Then she just sat there and reeked, and looked at me thoughtfully. Sometimes her eyes were kind, as if she had started trusting the judgement of the Supreme Court. Then I went to the woodshed and pretended to do carpentry.

That spring she often sat there and pulled her fingers through her blackhair. It was cold. I remember the northern lights the time when her eyes looked kind and I had gone across to the woodshed. Once I went half-way to the green house, my head bare, under the northern lights.

There were lights in the windows downstairs, but it was dark upstairs. Johannes must have gone to sleep in my bed. I think I was greeting.

They did not not want me to call them Mum and Dad. I called them Alfhild and Sven.

That felt quite natural.

When the deterioration had been going on for a while, Alfhild began shouting.

At first we did not understand what she said. Of course she had always been silent before, except when singing hymns, but the verses were so bred in the bone, there was no need to listen. But now it was all sung anew. Shouted anew, rather. Often she sat on the kitchen sofa and stuck her haun into her blackhair and twisted up her whole face

91

as if she had been quite despairing or happy, it was hard to see the difference, and bellowed.

The cheeks must have been just like a child's in the past, later they became like raisins, but when she bellowed one could sometimes see how it had been once, though she was twisted up. She bellowed, or coo-mooed, but not as if in pain, more like just being a bit melancholic or thoughtful and bawling while waiting to decide about speaking to us. Her shouting was not bad, in the sense of nasty, but rather as if she wished to pass on an important message she had pondered for a long time. Almost a heavenly message. Like the angelic trumpets in the Book of Revelations.

It was almost like the telephone-wires singing during cold winters and I thought it was a harp, strung from the stars: but the note was deeper, not truly heavenly, more like an animal's. Threatening and warm, she bellowed with an oddly deep voice, low, *mmmmmmmmmmmmmmmmmmmmmmmmmmmmmm*, then more loudly, MMMMMMMM, then *ooooooooooooooouuuuuuuuuuuuuuuooooooooohhhhh* MMMMM-MMMMMMMMMMMMMMMMMMMMMMMMMMMM*MMMMM-MMMMMMMMMMMMMMMM . . . MMMMMMM* . . . and then it died away, without her seeming to regret it. As if she had come out with something important and was now sitting there thinking it over.

At first I was not at all afraid. Then I felt a little afraid. It started, I think, with Sven Hedman saying quite briskly:

– Now we had better pay heed to your Mum.

She sang like a voice crying out. I was to heed my Mum.

Sometimes I thought: like a cow bellowing for its calf. I comforted myself with the thought that it was surely Johannes who was the calf.

It took a few weeks for us to ponder. Then after pondering for a long time we became dismayed.

Not so much for her sake. She had the stroke after the delivery of course. The second stroke must have been the exchange. In a way it was like two childbirths, which could easily lead to a stroke. And we did not get dismayed for our own sake. But we became afraid that somebody would hear something, and that they, the village that is, or the vicar, who was solemn but not very quick on the uptake, or the Sheriff, would perhaps come and make a fuss and take her away from us.

In the village they were quite hard of hearing of course. There was no hearing what Alfhild had become, her who was a bit bonnie and much-fancied reely.

Sometimes I thought that maybe it was I who had made her turn peculiar. But then I pushed that away: away all that! And then I thought it was Johannes.

I started thinking of how Johannes found it so easy not to take the blame.

Two mothers I have lost, and a father. Quite a lot, really.

One was in his grave and I knew him only through the corpse-picture (at that time I did not yet have the note-book). One sat about in the green house and became like a raisin when she saw me. And Alfhild, yes well she seemed so otherwise one had to regard her as lost.

Sven Hedman went the rounds of the village a bit and rooted about to find out if anyone had heard. Apparently not. They commented that we did not go to t'chapel. So Sven and I held a council of war and decided that one of us would always go to t'chapel.

We closed the door fairly carefully if there were any

well-meaning neighbours prowling about. Or we led Alfhild into the best room, that is the parlour, where we set out the greaseproof paper and pencil in front of her and I taught her to draw a map of Sweden. It was mostly the outlines, but I was always careful to mark Hjoggböle so that she would know were she was.

Then she did not howl.

In the main she was fairly regular. There was the howling in the morning, while Sven Hedman crammed the food in the sandwich-box and filled the flask, and then there was the bellowing in the evening. Some days it lasted maybe three four hours altogether, no more. When her mind was rueful it seemed to last longer.

Towards the start of spring she began bellowing words. Now that did get to be a problem.

Earlier on, Alfhild had got other problems. Not just that perhaps she was, possibly, a tinker, but other things as well. She had given birth to a boy before. That time she was lying-in at home and Sven had called the midwife, who arrived but had been in a hurry. Oddly enough it was the same story with Josefina. Anyway, the baby was the wrong way round, Alfhild had yelled like one dementit and in the end the neighbours had become almost dismayed and phoned the midwife who came in a hurry with her suction-bell and then, well into the third day and after much yelling, they got the baby out.

He was strangled by the cord. He had died just as his life began. They had christened him with the same name that I had been given later on, put him in the wee coffin and not taken his photograph.

Everyone kept corpse-pictures, even Josefina had one of

94

her first-born. I wish Alfhild or Sven Hedman had taken a photograph of this one as well. One wonders of course if we were alike, but the proof is buried in the earth, no picture was taken, and no inspection of ear convolutions by the doctors either.

Bellowed she did, that time too.

As spring drew closer, the words came, like growing shoots. It became a problem then.

They made almost coherent sentences. We minded this a lot.

The Hedmans' cottage was pushed into the edge of the forest, half a kilometre just across from the green house, the snow melted late that year, though summer would surely come, but all Sven Hedman and I could keep our minds on were the words Alfhild used.

These were quite strange words. It was as if now, in her plight, she had begun to use again a secret language she had once known. It was as if her life had been a kind of gigantic cauldron, inside it a bubbling blackness, almost like the barrel in Granddad's tar-burning pit, bubbles rose to the surface now and then and the bubbles came from low down, where her earlier life was. It was almost frightening. At the same time we began to look at her, that was something new. Everything came bubbling up. First it was just black and tough, but then there was the hair and the black eyes and the singing voice and something like loneliness in her eyes.

And then up came the strange and secret words.

One might think of the tar-barrel as her life, and the bubbles herself, and that she had become wrathful somehow, because before we had not listened. And that was why it was a secret language that she used.

It was like Eeva-Lisa's granddad, who had been hood-winked. If what Eeva-Lisa told was true.

People have been mistaken about them. And so in protest they use a secret language. I had learnt what the cats in the bed-end said, though they were varnished over. Animals I have always been good with.

But I never looked after Alfhild. No wonder she became sort of thoughtful.

She also began singing at night.

There was more singing during the night, and secret words during the day. At night like the heavenly harp, in the daytime secrets. It was alike, in a way. And because of that I never was truly afraid.

Sven Hedman became more pensive. Sometimes almost dismayed.

I have had two mothers. One never hugged me, but offered the cut-sugar. The other sang like a cat, but secretly.

Well I never. Well I never.

Later I thought the secret language was about trying to put her childhood into words. One cannot, of course, use ordinary words for this, only secret ones, no one can use the ordinary words.

Who can speak of what being a child was like. Nobody. Though it must be attempted. What would it be like if one did not.

For instance, Johannes tried, in Captain Nemo's library. Though it did not work of course, he did try.

I could have explained that to her: told her it was good to try. But I could not even make up my mind to do that. She got so wrathful then that the evilwords came out.

Both Sven Hedman and I became utterly dismayed when we realized. It was something to be ashamed of.

III

Because it gradually became clear to me that Nyland, in southern Finland, was the area from which *they* came, that is *they* who had a secret language, or who were like me, and very beautiful or very ugly, they came from the south and far away, though not from the Stockholm direction, I decided that this was where Alfhild came from.

Nyland, so much had emerged not only from *The Mysterious Island*, *Robinson Crusoe* and *The Jungle Book*, but also from the large family Bible with the pictures of the bare women being sucked down into the huge hole in the water, was a foreign place with palms and volcanoes with craters, enclosing underwater vessels.

However I had not asked Sven Hedman. He must have met her when she was very young, and he had not asked her either. What I mean is: if he had then she would not have become ugly.

Though one might ask oneself why it is so necessary to be beautiful.

After she had become a rather bonnie horse I pondered what Alfhild Hedman was like when she was younger. I thought of how she could have come up here by boat, along the coast. And how she had come because she had a secret to tell us. Of course, everyone has secrets, it is a matter of telling so that the rest do not comprehend, in order to get them to grasp it. There is a big difference between comprehending and grasping. But she had a very important secret, had travelled a long way not to give it away but make us grasp it.

But if the Supreme Court was right, then in fact I too come from the jungle kingdom of Nyland with palm trees and volcanic craters with underwater vessels inside, enclosing the Benefactor.

How difficult it is to perceive this. If I had, then I could have left the green house long ago, without sadness. But that I would not do.

First the singing, then the secret language, then the bellowing, then the ugly words.

She boomed like a foghorn.

– *Daaaaaaaaaaaaaaaaaaaaaaaaaaaddd iiiiiiiiiss foooouuuuu- uuuuuuuu* . . . *heeeeeeeeeeeeeeeeeeeeeeeeee iiiiiiiiiis iiiiiiiiiiiiiii- ii theeeeee hooooooooooooo'se*, and that was easy to understand. She was trying to sing us a parable. Some are in the Bible but not all. The Son of Man had scattered them about here and there, one of them a parable which Alfhild now passed on to us. It was like the homilies by the Blue Ribbon League. A harsh childhood and he came home and the child was ill and close to death and pale. *T'baaaaaaaaaaaaaaa- aaaaaaaaaaaaaaaaaaaaaallsheeeeeeeeeeeeeeeebaaaaaaaaaaaaaaa- aanged ooooooooon t'taaaaaaaaaaaaaaaaaable* . . . but then it got much worse, this was not how we sang in the Army of Hope. And then some additional terrible words, which were not bearable. It was dreadful. And then the song drifted off into a nice low mumbling, the usual kind, and the tone became a pure and clear bass, lamenting as if from the telephone-wires again, and so the dreadful, suddenly,

t'coooooooooooooooooooooooooooooooooooock heeeeeeeeee baaaaa-
aaaaaaaanged oooooooooooon t'taaaaaaaaaaaaaaable.

I looked at Sven but he just kept washing up, the same plate over and over again as if he was being very careful. For many minutes. He did not use to be that careful.

In the end he became so dismayed that he went out and chopped wood.

Alfhild sat there with her secretive little smile and fell silent, but touched lightly with her tongue both the roof and floor of her mouth as if to examine for any traces of the ugly words.

Afterwards she looked almost happy. Had she not been so dementit we could have sat together and chatted for a while. When she smiled like that all was well again. I recall that I really felt completely happy then.

When I was a child, thought like a child and dreamt like a child and had the understanding of a child, I often played the game of drawing by numbers. The game was in the *Norrie*. One had to draw a pencil-line between the figures, and then it became an animal. It used to be an elephant, or a bird.

Or it was in *Allers*. Both the *Norrie* and *Allers* were kept in the attic cubbyhole in the green house.

So one can draw lines between figures. Alfhild was a figure. I ought not to have drawn so quickly, to get to the elephant, I ought to have waited at every figure to grasp just what that point was.

That was the mistake. She was not an elephant but a horse. There is much to animals, it gets like that when one is unsure of being really human. Once, before the handing-over, a bird had got inside and flapped about and Josefina

99

had caught it in the gap between the winter-pane and the summer-pane, where the wadding was and the dead flies.

I started screaming, so she let it out. It was so scary with the wing-tips beating against the window-panes.

She must have been worried about the bird shitting, like the cat did on the wood-fired range. She was particular that there should be no dirtiness about. That was surely why I washed the leeches down by the burn, so that in the end they became completely clean. And the frogs which kept the cold spring clean. Though she pailed them out.

Sometimes I do not understand.

There is much to this about everything being completely clean. It was not like that at the Hedmans'. But then there are differences everywhere. The green house for instance, was not like the jungle in Nyland. One must understand that there were many things, which were unlike.

I had been standing there all baffled and deflated while the bird tried to get out, and then I had started screaming.

But it did not shit on the wadding. It shows there.

In June Alfhild screamed five hours a day. If a neighbour turned up for a chat, Sven Hedman went outside, almost a hundred metres away, and talked quite naturally, at a distance, so that nothing would be heard.

Increasingly, we lived the whole time with her shouting. That became almost the only important thing. Neither of us considered giving up. In time I think we really got to care for her a very great deal.

Maybe not such a very great deal as Johannes did for Eeva-Lisa. But we did not dislike her so terribly any more.

It is hard to explain. But it must have become some kind of love.

IV

The Hedmans owned, after his Dad who deaded in the timber forest, a summerbothy which was a timberman's hut, really. It was on the Mela River, which ran between the Holmsvass marsh and the Hjoggböle marsh.

In the end we took her there.

In the Hjoggböle marsh there were five islets and a reedbed with smallbirches which did not count. One of them was called Ryss Island, and seven Russians were buried there. They had been in the Russian army, which had been ravaging at the beginning of the nineteenth century, and they had strayed to Hjoggböle, but the villagers had killed them and buried them there. There were a lot of adders on Ryss Island and big-grown fir trees. These were not cut, because of the Russians and the adders, maybe, and had grown very big. These things meant that nobody went on shore. That was well known, and accepted by everyone.

Ryss Island could be seen far away from the green house shit-house, if the door was opened, but nearby from the timberman's hut on the Mela River.

We took her there.

We put her on the parcel-rack on the bicycle with the inflatable tyres which I had mended innumerable times with Sulision, that was what it was called, and trundled her away. Sven Hedman said that they had agreed about it, but I suppose it was rather that he and I were agreed, though for natural reasons she did not object at all. He

101

tied her in place with horses' reins which Nordmark had left behind in the byre at the time Sven was bull-keeper, maybe they had been used for leading the heifer, and she had been stubborn on the way there but afterwards much meeker, so they forgot the reins, in any case, they were still there. We had no horse of our own, nor a bull either any more, since that task had been taken away from Sven, who had since become taciturn and rather meek.

Alfhild smiled and howled all the time and seemed glad to get out. We went though the village. I believe they stared, but I cannot be sure. People could do what they wanted to behind their window-panes, of course, but I did not bother to look up. When we passed Lindgren's byre she said *fornicator* in a very loud voice.

Then we got to the road through the forest, and she fell silent. It took an hour to haul her along to the Mela River. It was quite a warm day.

We sat her down on the steps. She looked around and blinked, birdlike, with her blackeyes, baffled and quiet. She seemed to be in good heart. Be of good heart, said Sven Hedman to me, when he saw that my lower lip was quivering. Then I steeled myself. Really he must have been glad to have me with him.

That evening Alfhild and I fell asleep, but I woke in the night and saw Sven Hedman still up, sitting there reading the Bible, which was not his normal practice. He noticed that I was awake, and turned his head as if about to urge me to go back to sleep. But he said nothing.

I got up and went to sit next to him. Alfhild slept.

It was a very light summer's night. There was a slight watery mist over the marsh. You could see the tops of fir trees on Ryss Island, but not the huge middle branches reaching out and not trembling, like the fingers of God.

How could one actually become grown-up.

– She would surely be ill at ease in the cottage hospital, Sven Hedman said later, just before he carried me back to bed.

Imagine, he carried me, did not just tell me to.

V

He told me that there might be no need for him to work for the next few days. He could stay with Alfhild and me for a while.

The mist hung there still, almost every morning. Then it opened up, parted, it was quite dreadful and beautiful. Everything I can remember clearly from the time when I was a child is dreadful and beautiful. Ryss Island rose out of the parting mist, like a ship on its way towards me. It was on its way to me.

I thought of what was lying in the ground there, while the ship approached me through the mist and unswervingly kept its course towards me. There were adders as well. The fir trees were enormous and had not been cut for centuries.

It was important to be very attentive. Now it was quite close.

Sven was very deft at making porridge. I too became deft. Already on the second day Alfhild began to grow wilful.

She had no difficulties getting about, of course, but got worried when she was not allowed out. She seemed to long for the water out there. On the morning of the third day she was the first of us to wake up, and went outside bare-foot, dressed only in the light grey longjohns, which she liked sleeping in.

We got nervous when we woke and saw she had gone, but nothing had happened. She was sitting down by the lakeside with her hands in the water, looking for small fish.

We led her back in, quite calmly, and she sobbed for a while, and Sven Hedman almost did too.

– You had a beautiful Mum once, that you had, he said suddenly. And there was no responding to this.

He was strong and coarsely built and chewed tobacco constantly, but talked to me more and more, occasionally many times a day. I had planned asking if he longed for Johannes, but changed my mind and said nocht.

How could he have said it anyway.

On the third day we ran out of oatmeal. Then he said: I shall go and get more oatmeal.

He tied her to the leg of the bed with Nordmark's reins, and told me I had to keep watch.

There was nothing odd about being alone with her. That had happened before. It did not scare me especially. I think he was much more nervous himself. I noticed that while he was tethering her. He said, many times and quite unnecessarily, that it would not take long. He was just going in to the Co-op in Forsen to buy oatmeal and milk. He tested the knots lots of times, he was careful about that.

Then he looked at me, and pulled the bicycle with the inflatable tyres along towards the footbridge.

She looked well and happy when we were alone, but tugged

almost impatiently at the knots. She was a little unruly and did not sing quite the way she used to. In fact she sang or hummed almost angrily, almost in an evil way, looked at me with a wilful face and tugged at the reins. But the knots were very properly made and did not give.

They were properly made, so she looked at me in an evil way as if she were thirsty. One could see clearly that she wanted to drink. I gave her water first in the birch-bark scoop, but she did not want to. I told her what a short way it was to Koppra, and that Sven would soon be back, but she just waved her legs about and looked wilful, almost as if they had lots of clegs on them, which of course was not the case.

I was quite at a loss what to do. I could not think of what to say, but I had to come up with something to calm her, and so I said: – Calm down, Mum, he has just gone for the oatmeal. She looked at me rather oddly. I pondered what I had said. I had never called her Mum before. And she opened her mouth and began howling nicely.

I went over to the window and looked out over the lake. Then she fell silent. I turned and she was watching me then. I am not quite sure what it felt like.

So I began untying the knotted reins round the leg of the bed.

I led her down to the edge of the lake. There were no reeds.

She peered quite pleasantly into the water and looked for smallfish. I poked about with a dry stick and they rushed up and down like dementit creatures. I held on to the reins. Then she bent down and drank.

She did not bellow. I was not afraid.

Sven Hedman got back two hours later. By then I had tethered her to the leg of the bed again. He could not help seeing that the knots were otherwise, but he did not ask what had happened. He must have understood.

I said: She was thirsty but wanted water from the lake. Did you bring it back, he asked. No, I answered, I led her down so that she could drink by herself.

And then he asked nocht more.

He cooked the oatmeal porridge. In the night she started bellowing again.

I slept, but was woken up. I got up and said: She drank from the water of the lake by herself but was not at all unruly.

He had the Bible in front of him but it was not opened.

2

THE ADVENTURE OF THE HORSE

Her mouth breathing close to the icy seat
    lies Eeva-Lisa, my sister so big.
The moon-light net falling on the floor,
    legs in spasms like a slaughtered pig.

What slithers out of her is a fish,
    no real child, for God has refused.
The fishie screams and the fishie leaps,
    to punish the slut, who's been used.

I

The Hedmans have been done great injustice.

    Injustice has been done to Sven Hedman and injustice has been done to Alfhild Hedman.

    I was so near beginning to grasp it. But then she became a horse. And so she was taken away from us.

    But injustice has been done to them.

She did not like being kept indoors all the time. I sympathized with that and so did Sven Hedman.

It was the summer. There was green grass. And pines, and blaeberries, and water with smallfish. And light day and night. And Ryss Island like a ship.

Sven Hedman got more daring from that time on. It seemed that my taking her by the halter and leading her down to the lake strand, so that she could drink and look at the smallfish, made him more courageous. All spring he had gone about doing what he believed he ought. Cooked and wiped away the shit and sighed. In the end it probably got so he did not believe she was really human. Like sandpapering something away. He must have stopped believing that she was really human. But after I had led her and taken her to the water, he dared more.

He took her outside more and more then, to let her breathe.

She wore her longjohns and the fleecyboots and a knitted cardy. Maybe that was rather strange, since it was summer, but the fleecyboots had leather soles, so they did not get wet.

Over the blackhair she wore a headscarf. The overall effect was quite strange, until one got used to it. Then it seemed quite natural, and it was also good against the gnats.

I never got bitten by the gnats myself. It depends on what kind of blood one had got. Sven Hedman did not get bitten either.

We tied the horse's reins round her waist. That way she could walk about a little more how she liked. She pulled quite hard sometimes. Sometimes I was afraid she would pull me away with her.

Everything went so easily now.

There was no more fretting. It was odd. Alfhild pulled hard at the reins or lay down on the ground, it was like this or like that, sometimes she sang, and we listened and had a good time.

It was how it ought to be. Nothing worth mentioning or argufying about.

We had no boat, but I often fished in spite of the quite shallow waters. I went out from the wee spit of land, quite far out, up to my knees. There I stood holding the stick with the Extra Strong thread and a piece of board for a float, and the hook. It was irksome to get back on land to fetch the worms, so I kept the worms in me moo. The mouth itself was the worm jar, and of course there was no need to chat away when one was fishing.

When the crooked roach ate the worm off the hook, I just got the line in and pulled the worm-bait out of my mouth and fixed it on. It was as easy as pie, in its way, and Johannes and I had always done it that way before the exchange.

We anchored Alfhild by the reins under a stone and she sat there with her fleecyboots in the water, looking interested. When I caught something, then one could hear how happy she became.

Sometimes she sang a little. One could hear that she was well. The fleecyboots we dried on the steps in the evening sun.

It was as if Sven Hedman had started feeling that work was unnecessary.

The village was seven kilometres away, so nobody came out here. We were quite alone. One did not have to see the green house either. Sven and I went barefoot, but Alfhild insisted on her fleecyboots. We went along with her as she was, and that kept her quite calm. Some people like using fleecyboots in the summer, said Sven Hedman, and nodded and no more to-do about that. It was true too, we could see that. We went along with her as she was and she sat there and splashed with the fleecyboots and sang a little, and thinking about it, that summer must have been one of the best I have had.

Getting provisions became bothersome though. Sven and I met up in the kitchen to confer about provisions. Besides, it was not only the provisions we conferred about. It was in the kitchen he said that odd thing about Alfhild which I never got an explanation for. It was like the aunt in the tattie-cellar, with the chest and the letter which she read silently and then snorted and said:

– And that is what he says. And nothing more. It was maddening. This is just how it was with what Sven Hedman told me about Alfhild.

He said suddenly:

– I waited for her until she got out of prison.

I said Why was she in prison? It was unjust, he said, because she explained she had only wanted to kill the fish.

I asked How long was she in there for? He said I waited for her until she came out. How old was she then? I asked.

When she came out she was not as lovely as when she was taken in, he said.

Lovely, what a word.

– Who knows, I asked. Only the three of us, he said. I think you should know who your mother was.

Nothing more. It stands to reason I minded. Know who

your mother was. Just to let fly such a thing. And then say
no more.

Then he started talking about provisions. It was maddening.

II

July was very light and warm and quiet. We picked berries
and I stole milk from Albin Haggstrom's cows which were
out along the country road to Östra. My word, it was an
art. If they ran it splatted out. One had to strain for the
drops. I held the container in one hand and milked with
the free one.

Once a week Sven went to the Co-op in Forsen, which
really belonged to Vastra, and shopped for food. It was
mostly oatmeal.

He worried a bit about the money, he said.

During the nights, he and I often sat together, stealthily
reading the Bible while Alfhild slept. It was unbelievable
the things it said sometimes, if one was lucky. If one was
unlucky, it was like James Lindgren reading aloud.

Soon we will be able to pick cranberries, he said one
night. I realized that he planned to stay for a long time.

It was light all the time so we took no particular notice
of when we slept. It had to be when Alfhild did not sing.
One day Sven mentioned that dreadful thing, how once
they had told him that he was not to be bull-keeper any
more, and how this had been decided at the village
assembly, down by the milk table. He did not comment,
just mentioned it.

There were no more badwords from Alfhild.

111

The fleecyboots smelled only of lake water now.

One night Sven Hedman fell asleep at the kitchen table, his forehead against the wood, so he had a pattern all over when he stirred.

We started to walk her in the forest.

There was a small clearing for storing timber; grass grew through the pieces of bark and it was open and there was pine forest all around. Sven Hedman hammered a pole in at the centre, then he tied the horse's reins together so that they measured about five metres, tied one end round Alfhild and the other round the pole.

She could walk around quite freely then.

We were sitting on a fallen tree trunk and Sven had his snuff box in his hand and did and undid the lid as if to offer some, but of course only he wanted any. He explained that he did not believe she would like it in hospital, she would be ill at ease, he was convinced of that. Alfhild liked walking long distances in the fresh air, he insisted, that was obvious, and it must be unhealthy to sit there for ever with sour fleecyboots and have nothing better to do than to look for smallfish. I protested and mentioned that she was also curious about my fishing and had once dug up the worm bait for me from a cowplat, but then he responded that being exercised in the forest was good for her too.

It was so quiet and nice. There were birds as well. Alfhild walked slowly round the central pole, she limped slightly because the second stroke had gone to the leg a little too, but she walked well on the whole. We sat there, Sven and me, and we were surely both happy that she was so pleased. She was not beautiful of course, but kind, and did not sing ugly or evil, and, in a way, she had become

112

a horse. And since that happened we had started looking after her more and more.

And we liked her so very much. Before it had been dreadful. Now she had become a horse. And a horse must be handled well, and cared for and in the winter one must put the horse-blanket on properly if it was heavy going in the new snow and she was sweating: there was so much to a horse. One had to be very trustworthy.

Every day we took more and more care.

Sven curried her hair and I led her down to the lake strand so she could drink and look at the smallfish. She got lots of oatmeal-porridge with stolen milk and blae-berries and she ate and sang. She filled out and got well set. Really she did not look so caved in any more. Almost youthful.

Sven carefully restated that she was sure to be ill at ease in the hospital. That was why they were not to seek her oot agin.

She slept well at night. Sometimes she ran round the pole, wildly, as if she had become unco' glad. We dried the fleecies properly every day and tucked her into the blanket if she threw it off at night.

And it was as if everything had got meaning again.

They must have realized. Or maybe someone had noticed.

On the afternoon of 4 August Sheriff Holmberg came wandering along the path. His retinue included James Lindgren. We were sitting in the clearing as usual and Alfhild was bellowing merrily and having a nice time.

They stood still for a while, looking. Then they took Sven Hedman to one side and spoke with him. Then they untied Alfhild, and neither Sven nor I had any response to this. They held on to her very firmly.

She stopped trying to tear herself free after only a few minutes. And so they took her with them, leaving me to see to the last.

The following day they took her on the bus, first to transfer her to town. The idea was that she was to go to Umedalen next. To be taken into care, since she was considered dementit.

But she was not. When the bus stopped in Forsen to top up with timber for the gas-producer, she said or signed, it is unclear which, that she wanted to get out for a piss. In view of the long journey they had given her permission. She had then limped out into the forest, and disappeared behind a bush, thereafter not to be found again. The driver had by then got the gas-producer fire up and did not want to let it get cool, but drove on into Skellefteå, where she was to have taken the bus to Ume.

However, she had disappeared.

There was a general search. But Sven Hedman and I understood. Late at night, when the light was almost failing because it was August, we cycled to the Mela River. There she was.

She was sitting by the edge of the water, looking for smallfish and was perfectly calm but had not found her fleecyboots again. The good shoes she had lost. Her feet were in a terrible state. When we arrived she became pleased and beamed and grat a wee bit.

There was no bus until the next day of course so she had to sleep were she was.

It was the last night. Sven Hedman was sitting up at

the kitchen table where the black Bible was lying, but he only looked out over Ryss Island. I had gone to bed, but got up again and suggested we should steal a read in the Bible. But however much we searched we found nothing good this time. It was like a curse.

It was overcast and almost dark. In a way, the summer had come to an end and we could not see even one of the islands out there.

They took her away next day.

They took care to see to it she was pissed first, before she went, and she did not even try to run home again.

It was unbelievable that she had found the way. It was almost ten kilometres.

First she went to Umedalen, but then she was sent to Brattbygård, between Umeå and Vindeln. A month later, Sven Hedman and I travelled by bus to visit her at Brattbygård.

There were some dreadful ones there. It was smelly. There were several monsters and someone with crocodile skin and several idiots. They had been collecting all of those from Västerbotten. They had put Alfhild in a bed.

She was completely quiet. She combed her blackhair ceaselessly. Me she looked at steadily, as if she would almost have been able to say something, but we did not know.

That was the last time I saw her. She had her third stroke on 14 November. We made one single visit. It was dreadful.

One must try to make it have a meaning. Otherwise there is only despair.

We went to see her just once. On the way back in the bus I cried a little. Then Sven Hedman took hold of my arm, just below the elbow, quite gently, and finally I stopped.

Sven and Alfhild Hedman were done a great injustice.

I sometimes think that for a while I was close to seeing what kind of life she had lived. Surely it was a life after all. But there was never enough time.

III

THE ARRIVAL AT THE
ISLAND IN THE SEA

1

THE DISCOVERY OF THE
ANTHEAP

Very still now at last, Eeva-Lisa
sees a fish stuck in a net for a while.
Moonlight gleams and the floor is snowy
the fish crying like a helpless child.

Her awaited child did not come then,
there is a fish in the snow instead;
it is tied fast to Eeva-Lisa;
all flesh is grass, and shame is ahead.

I

It was a matter of drawing exact maps.

Franklin Island was sixteen nautical miles south of the
Nyland coast; the peak of the volcano could be distinguished from the outermost Finnish skerries. Sometimes
smoke could be seen. No one visited it, for fear of the

dead Russians who were buried there, and worry about the adders, which were plentiful.

The island was at a latitude of 61.15 degrees North, but the longitude was not established. That must be the explanation as to why it took such a long time to find it again. Fir trees grew on the island, uncut for hundreds of years, they were gigantic, the branches up to thirty centimetres in diameter. One could walk far out on them. When the volcano rumbled the branches trembled like the fingers of God.

You could see a long way when you climbed out on them.

There, in the water-filled core of the volcano was the last harbour of *Nautilus*. The vessel floated in the stillness of the volcano's interior, and Johannes had hidden there, in the library, to defend himself.

Nyland with its palms, its often impenetrable jungles and dangerous sand-fleas, where Eeva-Lisa's mother, paralysed and helpless, had been attacked by the rats during her last hours, that land from which came so many of my nearest and dearest, and of which I had been both dreaming and fearful, was a land to which I would never return.

But along the coast I found the island, the last harbour of *Nautilus*, where he had escaped into Captain Nemo's library.

'If the enemy cannot be found, then he must be recreated,' he wrote in one of his messages.

It was like a slight smile, almost sly but still friendly. It was as if he wanted to say: this is it, now you must start adding up. And when you have finished adding up you are to leave the vessel, open the ballast tanks and let the ship sink. All your life you and I have avoided this. But now I offer the knowledge as a gift. A sack of stones for you to carry for the rest of your life.

So there, add up, if you have the time.

Bonnie?

During his last hours I observed him intently. Bonnie? It is rather as if he were the unreachable part of my life, and then bonnie is surely not the right word.

The corpse-pictures. Dad's notebook. The return of the child found dead.

Johannes alive, me dead. Or maybe the other way round.

Thousands of notes. Quite a strange library, really.

'Eeva-Lisa wiped out my life when I wiped out hers. If one wipes out a life then one is the victim's executioner. But if both?'

'But about death, about death you know nothing. Nothing!'

The finest human thing: to live like a monster, far away, and to be the one who makes humanity visible. The joined-up one at Brattbygård.

Alfhild had become a horse, but even so Sven Hedman became like dementit when she died. In extreme danger and anguish perhaps one joins up. And if the other one had died then one had got joined to a corpse.

Was that why the corpse-pictures had to be put on the chest of drawers?

The big sin happened each Good Friday in the village when the Jehovah's Witness came round selling things although the Saviour was suffering on his cross and everyone ought to sit still and try to feel how dreadful it was.

The little sin arrived with Eeva-Lisa. Perhaps she had hidden it in the suitcase. The little sin was really such a good thought: that Johannes should become less nervous. And that Josefina should find again the child she once lost. And so she showed Eeva-Lisa charity.

But children grow up, of course. And those who are tainted with sin seem to become human. That must be why human beings are so strange. Though Josefina probably did not understand this, nor did the village. No, the tinker-like traits spread in the child, like a contagion of sin, though the parish had said that she was not a tinker at all, rather a Walloon, but came originally from the jungle kingdom of Nyland, which is said to have palm trees and secret illnesses and monkeys climbing in the trees and where no one realized that nearby there was the mysterious island with a volcano, on which grew big fir trees with branches like the fingers of God and with a peak of the volcano just like Benshill and in the winter it was covered by snow and snow-light and one could walk up the flank of the mountain in fleecyboots on the hard snow and everything was completely clean.

I saw her for the first time one day in October.

There had been a frost. She and Johannes had brought the skates, which Granddad had made, and gone on to the ice. Granddad had made skates for me while he was

Granddad, he was the village blacksmith of course, and knew how to. They had wooden soles and bowlt blades of wrought iron with a curl at the front tip, and then he gave them to me on my birthday. But which I had never had time to use.

Later they had been handed on to Johannes, that was quite natural.

I watched them from up on the road. Eeva-Lisa had Josefina's push-sledge, with frost-nails on, Johannes had the skates, and they were whooping. The whole lake was covered with new ice but they kept close to the strand, the outlet was open and down there the edges were yellow, as usual. I was standing up on the road, below Hedman's, and watched. They were like small ants, though Eeva-Lisa was bigger.

After an hour I went back in. That was the first time I saw Eeva-Lisa.

When I got home again, if that is the right word, I began thinking quite a lot about what Eeva-Lisa was like. I thought the whole evening long. There was not much to be seen from that far away, and the Hedmans and I had not cared to go to chapel during the time just after the exchange because they thought people looked. But even though I had not seen her from close to, it was easy to imagine how she was.

She had pale cheeks, beautiful slightly slanted dark eyes, a face like a cat and cascades of black hair which she pulled back into a tail. And nothing I saw later made me change that image, which proved to be absolutely right.

They seemed to play a lot.

I started spying on them because I thought it was important

to find out how much they played. In the spring it got easier, because then there was no snow to show up tracks. After May came the summer when Alfhild turned into a horse, but in September I began to watch out for them again.

I believe she understood that you have to defend the frogs, because I never saw her pail them out.

It was summer the first time I saw them down at the woodplaner's. Maybe it was May. I cannot remember any snow. August? They were sitting down by the washing jetty where I used to wash the leeches, where the water was black and no swimming was allowed because of those blood-sucking leeches. I went past on the bridge. They were sitting on the jetty. When I went past they fell silent, but Eeva-Lisa looked up. I was sure then that she looked just the way I had thought.

I bore no grudge at all because Johannes was sitting there. Grudging according to the prophet Ezekiel was almost a deadly sin. I told myself this several times during the next few years. But it was still hard for me at those times when I passed them sitting chatting on the jetty and they fell silent when I came along and Eeva-Lisa looked up.

One could think of oneself as a leech. One could think of that sometimes. One could be lying in the mud on the bottom, rolled up, but then start to move and unroll and so set out swimming upwards. Very simply, the way leeches swim, with wave-like movements. And then one would reach the surface of the water and see their frightened and nonplussed faces. Quite surprised, that is what they would be. And then one would turn, without saying anything, without batting an eyelid, and swim away, downwards, and in the end burrow back into the mud.

But there was no justice. Some were alone, others, by a sentence in court, got house and Eeva-Lisa and cat, and in some cases dog. Why was there no justice.

It was God's doing. And the Son of Man who was a laddie, who trachled along the roads of Palestine and nair-raly had time for anyone who already was not lonesome.

It was that she *confided* in Johannes. One lost all that of course. And he did not know how to look after her confi-dences, how to manage them properly.

Looking through the library one can see how much she did confide. She apparently told him of the calf pen. Though he has not understood what she is saying.

The two years with Elon Renmark in Långviken was something she would rather not speak about, but encouraged, she gave an account in a chatty way. She had been eleven years old when she arrived at Renmark's, a man who had shown her charity, and she was thirteen when she left. It had been a decent family. Elon Renmark was a big man with a turbulent temper who often cried violently. He was very sensitive, so he frequently beat his children, but gently and briefly. He used to cry with rage or with sentiment: for instance, he often told a story of a brother of his, during a funeral meal in honour of Renmark's first wife, who died from the cancer, how this brother had been given a pear in syrup for dessert. It was at the funeral feast. The preserved pear had been served in a sauce. The brother had then tried to lift the pear to his mouth with his spoon, but it had slipped off, and when he had tried to hunt for the syrupy pear it had been as slidderie as an unshoed horse on the lake ice, no way could he do it. He had chased it in vain all over the table with the funeral meats on it, while the guests had been anxiously watching the hunt. They had become quite amazed and sat there rigid. The table got quite untidy and the pear rather slochy.

His wife had died of the cancer and been in pain for many months and yelled loudly towards the end, and the story was very diverting. Elon Renmark in Långviken was of such a disposition that when he told the story he began laughing wildly, shedding violent tears as well. His whole face got wet. He was said to cry easily and be a good story-teller. He beat his children so that they would learn, but his heart was generally thought to be very warm and he had a sensitive nature. For instance, this was how he behaved when telling funny stories.

He was easy to like, because he had strong feelings, and those, it was thought, came of a loving nature.

His greatest interest in his spare time was keeping a look-out for poachers, at the behest of the parish, especially for elk poachers, but the task was taken away from him, though not the gun, when he shot a suspect hunter and only slightly wounded Fritz Hedlund from Gamla Fahlmark in the shoulder. Hedlund had been declared innocent, but one can think what one likes.

However, in this way his favourite pastime was denied him. Right from the start he had not at all disliked Eeva-Lisa, but that could have been misunderstood.

Elon Renmark lived in Långviken and had four
children, all boys, and one way and the other, for the
sake of the boys, he had regretted that Eeva-Lisa was
a girl. She did not especially want to dwell on this.
One night, about a year after she had arrived at
Renmark's, she had an attack of violent toothache. She
had been lying awake all night and the following day
had not been able to rack the hay as before. Instead
she had raked along the dykes or just hung around,
greeting. The next night she had not been able to sleep
again and had cried out loudly at times and the
following morning Elon Renmark's second wife, who
was of a calm disposition, the first one had died of
cancer and had shown a violent temper towards the
end, had cycled with Eeva-Lisa in to the dentist,
Östlund in Bureå, in order to get peace in her house.
Östlund originally came from Mjödvattnet but had
been trained as a dentist in Stockholm and had a good
reputation because his hands were so nimble.

He was also known for having a skull on top of a
cupboard, one could see that none of the teeth had been
worked on. This was by way of an example. It was
usually said that they were the only jaws in that room
which had not had a going over.

Eeva-Lisa had been seated in the chair and Östlund
had looked. He had been very displeased with her
teeth, but asked none the less where the pain was. When
she pointed he nodded in confirmation and said this is
it then. Then he had taken the pincers and pulled out
the illtreated tooth which hurt, and at the same time
three more illtreated teeth further in which would
surely soon start hurting too. Needs must, he had said,

127

though maybe neither Eeva-Lisa or Elon Renmark's second wife, who was of a calm disposition, had thought they were all that illtreated.

She bled a lot while they cycled back home, but it was of course only a matter of twelve kilometres to Långviken.

The bleeding did not stop, in spite of the bicycle trip. It bled for a whole day and she whimpered so much that the boys and Elon Renmark's second wife could not stay so calm any more. In the evening Elon Renmark had turned violent, almost to the point where he started crying, as when he told the story about the brother and the syrupy pear at his first wife's funeral, and practically sobbing, he had roared at her to stop yelling. The evening had passed in this way. When it was time for everybody to go to bed she was still bleeding and Renmark's second wife of the calm disposition had got worried about the blood and said that the mattress might be damaged.

Then he had taken her by the arm and led her out to the calf pen where there was a lot of dry hay, and said she could stay the night there if she liked.

She had been lying in the calf pen all night. In the morning Elon Renmark had got up very early and walked over to the pen and stood there for a long time, looking at her. Then he had led the calf out and come back and said nothing.

It was just about the only time she could remember him looking bonnie.

She had been as if the stuffing had been taken out of her body that morning. Her mouth felt odd and empty. She was ashamed because her teeth were so poor and because Östlund had to pull some out because they were illtreated. A year later she had the whole lot in the upper jaw pulled out by dentist Östlund, and got false teeth. She was thirteen years old then.

That is the story of the time she was lying in the calf pen. She had not disliked Elon Renmark, but he was violent and quick to tears and that must have been why he beat the boys. She had never been beaten herself. When he came to the calf pen in the morning he had looked bonnie.

And that is the story of how Eeva-Lisa had come to have false upper teeth.

It did not show that Eeva-Lisa had shop-teeth.

I think he is lying. She did not have shop-teeth. In that case it would have been noticeable. Instead she had a beautiful and slightly withdrawn smile.

This is the truth. If one has shop-teeth it shows. Everything else is slander.

III

The library: one of the first hints of what was to come.

He does not spend a single word on me. He has taken over the green house. It is like listening to a part of oneself calmly and almost scornfully speaking of another part as if he did not exist. The originally legitimate one. And closed his eyes to the fact that he was brought in, that I was there, just half a kilometre away, that all this was really mine, but that I had been cast out from the heaven of the green house.

I quote, in its entirety.

Up the slope above the green house was the outhouse containing the woodshed and the shit-house, or privy, as we were told to say. The privy was the place for reading the *Norrie* in peace, and it was built as a part of the woodshed. It was situated quite high up: if the door was open, one could see out over the whole valley, and the lake. One could sit there for a long time, listening to the mooing of the cows.

The outhouse was divided into two parts, separated by a thin wall: one half woodshed, the other privy. Sanfrid Gren in Västra Hjoggböle was the only one in the village owning two shit-houses: his privy was divided into two cubicles. He had became known for this. He did not have two because he was saved, everybody was of course, but because his father, who had built them, had been trying to appear prosperous. Two shit-houses signified not being a smallholder. This could be planned when the place was being built, wealth was not necessary: there was no shortage of timber. One built two shit-houses and hoped for treasure from the Lord. Then you just took it as it came.

For Sanfrid Gren it had come in its own little way, he had got the polio and become a shoemaker and been questioned by the Sheriff about that thing with the neighbours' lad, from Burstedts, who had been made to pull his trousers down. After he returned home he had become taciturn and just sat there with his lamelegs and droopy stomach and spent his time making fleecyboots. Thinking about it, there were many people in the village who became taciturn, what with one thing and another.

In any case he did have two shit-houses.

James Lindgren, who read from Rosenius, used to
say it was presumptuous to have two shit-houses. And
presumption was punished by God. And it was no help
then if the Son of Man tried to intercede and said
pretty please to God.

So, anyway, that is how bad it could be if one built
two shit-houses.

I was standing, on the occcasion which I am going
to recount to you now, between the aspens where
Josefina had put out the washing, including the knitted
things she called 'dolls' hammocks' and which she
refused to explain further although of course we had
no dolls, when I saw Eeva-Lisa walk up along the
path.

Perhaps I had thought about it before. But now I
decided at once. It must have been due to my thinking
about it before. Mostly to pass the time, but I got
nervous anyway. Very quietly I followed her up to the
back of the woodshed, and got into it by the back-
hatch. There was no snow, it was the middle of the
summer, so there was no telling by the tracks. The
aspens were nervous too, but they were like that all
the time, that was nothing to bother about.

I was wearing canvas shoes.

I heard her rummaging about with the newspapers
inside the shithouse, she must have been looking in
the pile of *Norrie*s for a Popeye she had not read. There
was no wall at the back of the bin, I had thought of
that before. There was sawdust on the floor of the
woodshed so I made no sound and besides I wore
canvas shoes. My heart was thumping right hard inside

me but of course that could not be heard, so I was not nervous about that.

Only Eeva-Lisa and me were at home. Josefina was cleaning the secondary school in Västra that day, because it had to be scrubbed before starting up. She was busy with that.

I saw the hole, the one to the left, and saw that Eeva-Lisa had sat down there. It was sort of round where one could see her bottom. I shall never forget it, because of course earlier I had been thinking about it a bit. And now one was at last allowed to see.

I had always wondered what she looked like. It was very round, really the way I had thought it would be, though maybe even more beautiful. There was no harm in looking, I suppose, and it was almost more beautiful than I had thought, though it was certain to be sinful. The question was if it was a mortal sin, like going to communion without being saved, that is to say the kind of mortal sin which the Son of Man could not even intercede about, and which made for burning for ever. Perhaps I would have done it even if it had been a mortal sin, that is how much I had been thinking about it, it was almost enough to make one dementit. But now anyway it was just as round as I had thought, though even more beautiful.

Then I saw how her bottom disappeared from the hole after she had peed. I stood there, breathing with my mouth open, so no one could hear.

And then, suddenly, the dreadful thing happened.

I saw that hair of hers, the long black head of hair that was so beautiful, saw how it was sort of lowered down through the hole. And then the whole head, carefully. And how she turned her head and looked me straight in the face. I stood there among the cut logs with my feet in the sawdust and I was as if turned into a pillar of salt and could not move.

We looked at each other for just a brief moment. Nothing was said. Then she carefully pulled her head out again, and I could hear her put the wooden lid back on. There was a rustling, as if she was putting a newspaper away. She opened the door and closed it again. She came out.

But she did not go round to the back.

After just half an hour maybe – it might have been less – I got out through the back-hatch again and went down to the house. She was sitting on the steps, waiting for me. She did not say anything, but looked at me kindly. It was almost as if it had been a kind smile, but she did not smile and that was good.

Then she went back in. Josefina came back from the cleaning. Afterwards Eeva-Lisa never ever said anything about it, but looked at me kindly sometimes. I think that in a way it was the first secret we had together. I never asked her what she thought, but when one has a secret together, one which was so dreadful at first that one almost died though it was quite small, then one joins up a little. And afterwards it is never the same. And then the other secrets come along.

He has drawn a line through some of the sentences. But they can be read anyway.

There is another page full of writing about the same event. There he is trying to be more jocular, as if getting down to some serious lying.

I once saw them quite close by when I went along with Sven Hedman who was going to install a new stove in the chapel.

They did not know I was watching. I was standing behind the window in the chapel. They went round the wild-rose hedge, down towards the cold spring and Eeva-Lisa was carrying a pail in her hand.

Thinking of someone just about all the time is like lying in an antheap, it is dreadful, one imagines, one gets stuck, like on a tar-stick, everything just goes round and round, just because it is so hopeless, it is impossible to think of anything else, one is sure she is walking around laughing, and it hurts. Why does it have to be painful. Everything to do with Eeva-Lisa is food for thought, from her bitten nails to her mouth. There may be other things to be done, cooking meals for instance, or anything, but one is still like a flea on a tar-stick, no, a flea dies of course, but one is forced oneself to live on, thinking, thinking, but it hurts. One cannot grasp how it can be so dreadful. Waking up is dreadful but sleeping is good because one is allowed to touch her and chat to her, but after that the worst thing is being awake.

If only she had not come.

What I mean is: one is driven dementit. Though it is just by thinking, one ought not to, it gets like in an antheap.

She can be seen from far away, from the other side of the burn and one cannot go across and talk, not even a chiffin, because it would surely show that one was lying in an antheap. And I wish she had never come, because it is like discovering an antheap inside, and it stays there, one

134

is never free again if it is there, inside, and one is spurned and not allowed to sit aside her, except that once with the tulips on the dress material, and in the end in the woodshed at Hedman's, but never in the elk watchtower for instance, no never there, not there.

I believe I could almost have managed the exchange, if only she had not come. She was so bonnie. If only she had not come.

My head hurts.

When my head hurts I think about the animals to make it stop. The cat who shat on the iron range, it had been jumping for a bumble-bee before it was sent away. The fledglings which did not understand that we wanted the leaves to keep them warm in the night, but died, though it surely was not as if we had murdered them. The frogs in the cold spring, when I was the animal keeper and defended them. The calf in its pen, which made Elon Renmark look bonnie. The horse, who walked round round and felt well.

Have I forgotten anything? Surely. The bird between the window-panes and much more besides.

I was standing in the chapel and heard Sven Hedman pottering about with the stove. I was standing so close to the window, as if I was not at all afraid of being seen. They went round the wild-rose hedge and disappeared.

I forgot the birds in the rowan. Or maybe it was the lucky tree I forgot.

'If the enemy cannot be found then he must be recreated.'
Yes, he might well say that.

2

THE ENEMY IS
REVEALED

Grabbing the fish round the neck then
   beating it to stay still and dead.
Thumping on the wall in the moonlight
   eggshell-like cracks in the fishie's head.

God, let the fish remain silent,
   help me hide my shame in the night.
Now, make the fish stop his wriggling,
   his twisting when I hold him tight.

I

Afterwards I ought to have thought: it is strange how
things happen. One gets a knock, but nothing is hopeless.
Sometimes it is so dreadful one just wants to die, but when
everything is at its most dreadful one knows that somehow
one is still alive. It can be felt. It burns, and remains like
a small burning point of pain. And so one lives, if it is
not carelessly lost.

There is no need to believe that everything is very happy, only that there is always something better than death. And one should also keep the source of pain. No point in crawling away to hide and forget, the way both Johannes and I did. Because what is left then. If nothing is kept, then of course nothing remains. And then there is no meaning at all in any of the pain.

Then it would only have been hurting. Quite meaninglessly. And if so, one would just have been a quite meaningless human being.

Perhaps it is the source of the pain which is the proof that one is human.

I remember the parable from the Epistle of St John in the New Testament, one of the places Sven Hedman and I found in the Bible that night.

This is the parable. It is Jesus telling the parable of the donkey and the empty jar of honey.

Jesus told his apostles that the donkey Eeyore had a birthday, and to please the donkey his two friends, Piglet and Pooh, hit on the idea of each giving Eeyore, who was rather quiet and thoughtful and often sighed heavily, a present. That is why the pig called Piglet bought a balloon, and Pooh Bear a jar of honey. However, walking along to see Eeyore, Pooh Bear got hungry and tasted the honey, which was good to eat; so before he had arrived the jar was empty. Piglet ran along eagerly at his side with the balloon in his arms, but stumbled suddenly and fell, and the balloon burst and became just an empty cloot.

So, when they arrived, all that remained was a jar without honey and a burst wee cloot of a balloon.

When they handed over their gifts the two friends told

Eeyore the donkey what had happened and felt ashamed. Eeyore looked over the gifts for a while with his usual sad eyes, and the two friends felt quite at a loss, what with sadness and shame. But then the donkey took the balloon-rag and put it in the pot. And then, after thinking a little about it, he pulled the rag out of the pot again. And then put the rag back in. So then the donkey, Eeyore, said happily to his friends, this is a very useful pot to keep things in. And this clootie balloon is a thing to keep in the useful pot.

And they understood suddenly that what they thought was nothing, really was something, and they became very happy.

That was the parable about the donkey and the jar of honey. One gets a knock, but all is not hopeless. One can keep that which hurt, and it becomes worth more than happiness.

So it was with the Bible. There were things to find, if you looked. And these things can help when times are hard. Of course everyone is an empty jar or a burst balloon which can be of great value, as Jesus told his apostles.

II

After Alfhild had become a horse and been moved away and died at Brattbygård, I lived alone with Sven: and so it happened at about one in the afternoon on 4 June 1944 that Johannes, whom I had often seen but had never played with because of Eeva-Lisa, came up to me in the long break and told me to hurry up with my margarine sandwich and my milk and come along to the back of the school, where the wood-pile was. The school was a Grade B-2.

I did as he asked me, but he was rather silent, and only said he would talk to me on Sunday, after the midday service. I was to meet him in the forest above the privy belonging to the green house. He was going to show me something, he said, but would not say what it was.

It did not seem right to say no. I just nodded and asked no more. Then he said a bit more: If ye hurry yersel' after chapel you will be the first.

That did sound odd, but I nodded and then he left.

The black circle after the May Day bonfire was still a burnt roundel and the grass had not grown through yet. Johannes was sitting on the chapel log-chest right at the back, he slunk out first. I was alone, because Sven Hedman was now just about the only one in the village who kept away from the Saviour, a fact which was interpreted in different ways but was not thought too well of. I walked quickly.

He waited for me to come.

He was wearing the brushed cotton shirt and the short trousers and I recognized the shirt, but said nocht. When I arrived, he just nodded upwards along the road, or rather the wide path, which went up over the front of Benshill, and apparently wanted us to walk up the way. And so we did.

I knew the forest well. One could observe things from in there. And hide from enemies inside it.

I had once drawn the forest as carefully as the green house. Drawing maps was important. I had taught Alfhild to draw maps of Sweden, showing Hjoggböle, at the time when she was about to become a horse. She had drawn about ten or fifteen of them, but if I did not put in the dot

for Hjoggböle she got angry and bellowed. It was important to put it in, otherwise she would not calm down and
draw. I made maps of practically everything, usually of
the marsh with the islands marked, and was careful about
Ryss Island where I had never set foot, because of the
Russians and the adders: I drew it especially carefully with
the Bay of the Intruders and the volcano and the path over
the pass with the fallen rock and all the rest.

I had also drawn the forest above the green house in
detail many times.

A road went from the chapel, more of a path really, and
it became narrower and narrower, and a path, quite simply.
Johannes went ahead of me, without a word or a gesture
to reveal his purpose. His hair was blonde and he was
wearing a brushed cotton shirt and canvas shoes. Josefina
must have altered the shirt and let it out, so that the material
would not go to waste. I looked at his ears from behind.
There had been a lot about them in the papers, it was
jokingly said in the village, no ears can have been as
carefully examined by the doctors and the Supreme Court
as these ear convolutions on Johannes and me.

I too wore canvas shoes. Just the same. But nobody had
taken any notice of that. There are differences between one
similarity and another.

He walked quickly, and turned around now and then,
but he was not really looking at me. It was as if he were
looking over his shoulder. But of course no one was there.

At last I asked what he was looking for. He did not
answer. The next time he turned I asked again. He
answered then, looking straight ahead:

– The Enemy.

He might have been playing, or become dementit. But

I could hear from his voice that he was that serious. And dementit he was not. I was sure of that, because otherwise it would have been talked about in the village as with Ernfrid Holmström, who had once gone dementit and been carried off to Umedalen. He had gone dementit, no question. The whole village knew at once. They had tied him to a chair in the best room, it was necesary although he was just twenty-four years old and well liked by everyone for his modest manner. All the women in the village who were big with child had been warned against looking at him: if they did, the child in the mother's womb would get a fiery mark on its forehead. But only Malin Häggström was carrying, and they kept her away, that was not a problem. Ernfrid Holmström came back from Umedalen six months later and was just as usual. Malin Häggström gave birth to an ordindary child without a fiery mark, but she had been worried even though she had been kept away.

But Johannes in any case was not dementit. Obviously one wondered just the same.

We walked quickly up the mountain, I was sweating in the end, but I did not want to get behind like another auldhorse. We went up and up. But just two hundred metres away from the top, where the elk watchtower stood, Johannes pointed in under the rockface, at the mouth of the cave and said:

– Go in there.

And that of course was the cave of the dead cats.

There were three cats in the cave, all dead. The first one had been picked quite clean. It must have been a girl cat, because she was so beautiful. She had such a beautiful white head. We leaned her up against the wall, that is, against

141

the inner wall of the cave, so that she could see through the mouth of the cave out over the forest and down to the village. It is important to have a view when one was dead. The other two, which had not been picked so clean were rather unpleasant to look at, so we buried them under the earth floor inside the cave.

But that had happened before the exchange, when we spent a lot of time together. That had been five years ago. The odd thing was, the catgirl was still there, just the way she had been that time when we propped her up. Now she was picked completely clean and even more beautiful than before. She sat looking out over the forest and the valley and just looking calm and bonnie.

Johannes sat with his back against the wall at the entrance. He was so serious he seemed almost nervous.

– I thought you should know too. They come here every Sunday afternoon after chapel and they will be here soon. When chapel is over.

I did not understand a thing, so he said to clarify:

– I realized something odd was going on, when he came all the way from Västerböl and he was surely not one for chapel before. And not here. So there was something odd about it.

He nodded energetically.

– Who? I said.

– The Enemy, Johannes said.

It must have shown that I understood nocht. So he explained:

– He takes Eeva-Lisa with him and they walk along the path here. And then they go to the elk-tower. It is dreadful.

The catgirl was looking calmly out over the valley and

142

looked bonnie. I wondered if she had heard, but she pretended that nothing had happened. One does that if one is dead, that is natural. I thought as hard as I could, but did not get it.

– Does she go along of her own free will? I asked and hoped he would say no, because then I would not have understood a thing and it might have been a game.

– They go there and canoodle, said Johannes. I wanted to tell you, because I have seen that you are on guard.

He had seen. Or maybe Eeva-Lisa had said something. I just stared at the dead catgirl.

– You are the only one I am going to tell, he said, because we must defend Eeva-Lisa.

Then I understood. And I nodded, because now it was obvious, it was just as important as the frogs. It was no more than a minute before we saw them come.

I recognized him straight away.

He lived about two kilometres away in Västra but was well known, he played centre-half and was generally well liked, almost like an example for the young, people said, even though it was not certain that he was saved, because people in Västra of course were of weaker faith than us in Sjön. Johannes was right, it was very odd that he had started to go to chapel in Sjön. He was quite heavily built and had a liberating kick which had saved the team in many a time of trouble. They passed by only ten metres below the cave of the dead cats.

It was him Johannes had called the Enemy.

They had started playing football in Västra many years ago, when somebody had the idea of trampling together a ball of paper, using pages from the *Norrie* and tying round

143

it with string; and they had carried on kicking it about until they got a real ball and began to play. His name was Lars-Oskar Lundberg and he was about twenty-five years old, centre-half because of his liberating kick and well known in several villages, though in Sjön the youngsters kept quiet about him if somebody grown-up was listening, because of course football was sinful. That must have been why Johannes smelled a rat when he started going to chapel in Sjön.

Naturally, we never played foothball in our village, and quite apart from the religion, nobody wanted to get the leens trodden all over.

I forgot at once that he was generally well liked, and began thinking of him as the Enemy. He held Eeva-Lisa's hand a little awkwardly and spoke in such a low voice we could not hear. They did not look up towards the cave. She wore her best dress, the one with tulips.

So they passed. We left the cave of the dead cats together, and followed them cautiously.

They never looked behind. I do not think they could imagine themselves followed. When they disappeared round a bend we went forward cautiously to the next one, but because Johannes knew were they were going we did not worry. They held hands almost all the time.

It was dreadful. I do not know what was so dreadful. It was like the aunt down by the bus, she who had given me a hug even though Eeva-Lisa was watching. That too was dreadful, but not as dreadful as it used to be. When Alfhild had been sitting in her bed at Brattbygård it was dreadful but not that way, it was plain dreadful. This time it was dreadful differently.

Johannes must have felt just the same. But that was the

way with him, I never dared to ask anything, though he was like a part of me. Absolutely joined but so totally strange a half.

Why did it have to be like this. I often thought: why was it necessary.

From perhaps a hundred metres away we saw them climb up into the elk watchtower on the top of Benshill. It was well built, timber was not a problem.

They stayed up there an hour. We could not see them, because the railing was a metre high.

I am almost sure I know what it was like. He must have been shy. And she was soft and used to being on her own. So she stroked his cheek. And because they were so high above the ground and the air was so warm, with a light breeze, they floated as if through the clouds, and left everything behind and below, then at last they were not afraid.

I know that. She was wearing her tulip dress.

Then they climbed down.

I have never been afraid of dying. But I have never wanted to die, because first I want to make it all add up.

First added up and completed. Then one can stop dying. So that must be why I am still alive.

We said nothing on the way home, Johannes and I.

Afterwards we sat in the cave of the dead cats. We were there, and the nice little catgirl with its white head which looked so thoughtfully straight out over the forest and the valley and the village where I lived once.

145

What might she be thinking about us. What might she be thinking.

III

From that moment Johannes and I met almost every day. So I should know.

In Captain Nemo's library he wrote down something of what he knew himself. Most of it is true. But the hardest, how to defend Eeva-Lisa against the Enemy, that seems to have got forgotten somehow.

Eeva-Lisa was quiet but happy during the next few days, she did not talk to me much. It was as if she felt shy, or had lost interest. It must have been the Enemy's fault, not hers. It was understandable how it could be. Josefina had no idea and we had agreed not to tell her about Eeva-Lisa and the Enemy.

They probably spent a few more times in the elk-tower. But then something happened. I was the one who discovered it. I went up there one Thursday night and saw it.

Somebody had sawn down the tower.

It was badly done, so I realized at once who it was. I think he had been sawing with an ordinary handsaw; first one of the corner posts had been sawn through, without pinching, because he had wedged it well, and then two more posts, but less carefully, because there where several chipped bits where he tried again. Then the tower had been pulled from side to side until it fell, or rather it had been toppled over, as if by

146

somebody enormously strong. And it had fallen over on its side.

So this tower has had its last visitors.

I cannot understand how someone so weak could be so strong. He must have done it at night. He must have been quite frightened when he did it, or angry.

Kalle Burström discovered it a week later. Then it got about. I could see that Eeva-Lisa was afraid when she heard. Maybe that is why everything between her and the Enemy ended so quickly. They had no tower to be in any more. And then they must both have understood how it fitted together, and so it was all over.

It was discussed down by the milk table and it was generally agreed that it was a villanous act. Though nobody could work out how it fitted in.

The centre-half stopped coming to chapel in Sjön only a month later.

What can one say. He just disappeared. It was as if he had never existed. What can one say.

And I never said anything about this to Eeva-Lisa.

I was there when Sven Hedman's Mum died. It was the cancer. Sven Hedman did not want to lay the corpse out himself, so I had to help, with one of the neighbouring wives.

When I speculate that the exchange may have been just, and try to think that the Supreme Court and the doctors with their ear convolutions had been right, though they could not be, then it was really my own Granny.

She just coughed suddenly, breathed a few times and died. I stayed in the corner, because Sven Hedman sat in the kitchen and was depressed, so I was allowed to be in there. When we arranged the sheets I could feel that she had been covered in sweat, though she was already almost cold. The sheet slipped away so I could see one of her breasts. It was the first time I had seen a woman's breast. Then the neighbour's wife covered it up. It was solemn and not at all dreadful.

I did not really understand that death could be like that, still and thoughtful and solemn. And it was so strange, as if a dead person just by being a bit sweaty and cold at the same time was trying to tell what it was like to be alive, or how it had been. This was what one was like in life, but she never told me until she was dead.

It was I who had sawn down the elk-tower. But I could never be bothered to be properly ashamed about it. One carries out one's villanies, but if one is supposed to be ashamed of everything, what kind of life is it.

I did not do it at night, he is wrong there in what he has written, he always tried to write in some mistake so it should not be too obvious. But I did do it with a handsaw.

I suppose he could see that from the cutmarks.

There is a lot in the library about guilt. But it can surely not have been my sawing down the elk watchtower which frightened the Enemy away from her.

Afterwards autumn came. And winter, the worst in living memory. And then of course they could not have gone to the elk watchtower.

So that guilt is wiped away.

Guilt and tears. And the Son of Man was nowhere to be

found. Only Captain Nemo, if he is still prepared to help a poor thing like myself, like us, I mean.

Benefactors are in great demand.

IV

Winter came early that year.

It started snowing in September, which was not out of the ordinary, of course, but the odd thing was that it went on and on. By October the snow was half a metre deep and it was cold, the stevedores in Bure harbour were laid off a month early and Sven Hedman was troubled, because the fat money pooch looked like the cloot for straining coffee, as he jokingly put it one of the few times he tried to joke. All the land along the coast was laden with snow, and those who went away to fell timber knew there would be heavy padding and a lot of snow inside their cagouls. But worst of all was the horses getting up a sweat and then maybe catching a cough. Sven Hedman had no horse, that is true, but he thought a lot about how it was worst for them.

I had started to visit now and then in the green house, when I knew that Josefina was away on big bakes. I realized that when she saw me she fell silent, her face all strange, and that there was talk in the village. So better that way.

Johannes had never said anything about the sawn-down elk-tower. But Eeva-Lisa had become quite otherwise.

She kept herself to herself most of the time and was not as merry as she used to be. Once when I got there she was sitting in the sofa, sobbing away, and Johannes was sitting next to her, saying sweetie, you. It was hard to understand her. In many ways she was just as before, and I remembered how smooth she was to touch if just for fun one took hold of her arm. She always smelt of soap and was smooth. But now she was otherwise, no question. She had filled out a little, not so that she had got fat, but she was plumper, somehow rounder, anyway, she had put on a bit. I used to say, 'You look sonsie,' when I came in to see her; it was well meant, but then she looked at me as if I had said something unkind. So I only said that she looked sonsie twice.

Though it was what one was supposed to say to be nice to someone who did not seem to have any difficulty keeping their food down.

But she was ill-tempered. She really had nobody to talk to, apart from Johannes and myself. And after the tower had been sawn down, and the Enemy disappeared just as if he had been something Johannes had thought up for a scare, or to get rid of his shame, the silence closed in on her still more.

Once when I came she was alone at home.

Johannes was gone to the Co-op, or Koppra, as it was really called, but she let me in anyway. I think she wanted to talk. She made me sit on the sofa and showed me her knitting. She had got the notion she would teach me how to knit, and at the time I did not bother to tell her that, while it lasted, Josefina had taught me to knit ovenmitts.

Casting on she would do herself, because that was too hard for me, she said. And then I was allowed to try.

It felt really strange. She was sitting so close. She was wearing a dress she had made herself, she told me. It was the first one she had made herself, a whole dress all on her own that is, from buying the material to drawing, cutting and sewing up. She had planned to make it a surprise for her Mum, or Josefina Marklund, as she called her when she was angry, or sometimes Marklund, when it was very bad, Mum was to be pleasantly surprised that she had been able to. That was the idea.

The material was so smooth. I was allowed to touch it. It was the best dress with the tulips. I looked at the flowers for a long time and felt them. The tulips were turned upside down, they were growing with the flowers pointing down so to speak. I asked why she had done it that way, usually they grow upwards. But then she became somehow otherwise again, and said that Josefina had noticed too. She had happened to turn the flowers downwards when she was cutting, so the flowers happened to grow downwards.

That surprise had been nothing much worth writing home about, Mum had said.

Then I said it really looked more beautiful like that. And that I had heard that there were flowers growing downwards in foreign places, not near Stockholm, but in Nyland, where there were palms as well; it was far away, to the south of Nordmarks, if looked at from that direction.

There was no need to think that all tulips were alike, I said.

And then she stroked my hair.

– Your hair is as black as mine, she said, but your soul is quite white.

She thought I was good with my hands. She took hold of my hands to investigate them. She said the inner surfaces of my hand were nice and soft and that must be why I was so good with my hands and learnt so quickly.

That was all.

Afterwards, I have often thought of us sitting there,

practising knitting. And I imagine we did not at all care about the knitting, neither of us, but that instead both us could hardly breathe. It is difficult to explain to somebody else who has not experienced it. And if I could have become somebody else, as brave as Johannes, who could sit there and say sweetie, you, in the way I had always dreamt of, but could not, then maybe I would have leaned over against her arm. And my cheek would then have felt the material of her dress, on which the tulips grew downwards, towards the earth, or soil, as they said in chapel. And we would have been like brother and sister, who had found their way down to the soil where we and upside-down tulips alone could grow, and then we would have been lying there, rolled up like the leeches in the mud down in the burn, never never wanting to swim up or grow up, and big sister and I would have kept our secrets, but not from each other, and neither of us would ever leave the other behind.

V

She was having a bad time with Josefina, I realized that. Because they had both hoped for so much, they must have come to hate each other. If they had not been so full of hope, things might well have worked out better. Nobody really tried to understand Josefina, because she was generally respected anyway, and that makes for great loneliness.

I noticed that when I said all that about the tulips, it somehow made Eeva-Lisa happier. I say 'somehow', because nowadays she could never be truly happy. But it was something of the kind.

When I was a child there was a lot which was *somehow*.

When something was somehow it took a lot of thinking to understand; nothing was as it seemed.

Mum froze over, and it must have got worse when Johannes and I were exchanged back. That was the worst, and then it carried on being the worst, and so she froze over. It is surely worst for those who freeze over. Like Eriksson from Fahlmarksforsen who got the pine tree on top of him and got pinned down and had written *Maria, you sweetie* . . . with his free finger. Mum had maybe frozen like that, though she had not even a free finger and no snow to write in, and not even anyone to address *you sweetie, you*. Sometimes I thought that she dreamt of being allowed to crawl into the wound in the side of the Son of Man, and get warm and feel nice and thaw out. And not have to think of what had happened. But the Son of Man was not the one to stand by you when you needed him, she too must have realized that.

Wherever she looked there was guilt. Johannes was no angel boy, and if the chosen one was not, then the outcast was sure to be that much worse.

So Eeva-Lisa was the one who got the evileye. She bore the punishment. Certainly, she was clean and properly dressed and got as much food as she wanted, Josefina was particular about those things. And surely the mean little sum paid by the parish had nothing to do with her having been taken in.

Nocht. Josefina always stressed this carefully. When she got on to the subject she was careful to stress it. When the Son of Man would not open up the wound in his side, then there was nothing for it but to stand outside in the cold and put stress on.

I thought a lot about Eeva-Lisa as the winter came on.

The snow fell and fell, in the end we were enclosed like summerflies in the wadding between the windows, the wadding which I was sure God had put there as soil for flies. God was goodhearted with flies and let them have wadding laid out and allowed them to sleep on it till May, when he swept them out, with people he was nairraly mean, I shall never get to understand God.

One day at the beginning of November I met Eeva-Lisa down by the post-bus. I was to get the sack at the door and take it up to Sehlstedts', where the post was spread out on the sofa so that everyone could come and collect it. I used to get the sack and take it up there. But Eeva-Lisa never went to get the post. Now she was there. It was as if she had been waiting for me.

And she said: You must help me.

It was me she wanted to help her. Nobody else. Not even Johannes, that was the strangest thing of all. It was as if he had not existed though he was so bonnie and well liked by everyone. And I did not bother to ask about it. But often I think that it must have something to do with what I said about the tulips.

She wanted help. This was how the dreadfulness really started.

The next day she walked through the unploughed all the way to Sven Hedman's. I was at home alone, because Sven was out sawing ice for the ice-house of Petrus Furtenback, in the village he was that one who had once been proved to drink lager. But then, it was often said, what could be expected from someone with a name like that.

I told Eeva-Lisa all this when she came and laughed out

154

loud myself. I think she understood how nervous I was. No, not nervous, but scared. I told several stories about Petrus Furtenback. She did not laugh.

I got more and more scared. We were sitting in the kitchen and I urged things on her, but she would not take a slice of scone with a lump of sugar, and no cranberry drink.

Then she said: I think I am with child.

In the family Bible in the green house – the Hedmans did not have one – there were pictures I often looked at, though surely they would have been sinful in any other book. Sinfulness almost always had something to do with women, because in their way they were so easy to like, almost bonnie. There were for instance also sinful pictures in the Åhlen and Holm mail-order catalogue, which one of the Burstedt boys had been caught looking at in the shit-house when he had forgotten to put the inside hasp on the door, and afterwards in chapel with everyone listening, he had to ask God's forgiveness because he had sinned. But then the catalogue was not the Bible.

The Bible could not of course be sinful anyway, it was one's own filthiness that made the Bible sinful. There was a distinction between two kinds of sin, sins which could be forgiven and mortal sins for which one would burn without hope. I do not know if it was a mortal sin to foul the Good Book with sinful thoughts, but after the eldest Burstedt boy had confessed in the chapel his mother had asked the preacher if this was a mortal sin, all this about having sinful thoughts, and perhaps actions, she had not been very clear on this matter, about the bra advertisements in the Åhlen and Holm catalogue. But the preacher, it was

Bryggman, had replied to this with a denial. The eldest Burstedt boy was forgiven.

Or rather: at first he had hesitated and thought it over and said it depended. And the mother had started greeting and wanted it not to depend. Then he had said it was an ordinary sin after all, which was forgiven now. And then she had praised the Lord and gone home and mucked out the pig-sty.

The Bible must be worse after all. It was hard to get to sleep afterwards and every time I prayed a lot to the Son of Man.

Not that I thought it out properly, but women seemed to be a temptation just by being so bonnie. There were pictures in the Bible, in the Old part that is, of the Flood, with the seawater washing over almost bare women, who probably drowned. Like Erik Lundkvist from Gamla Fahlmark, when he drowned at Sjöbosand and his wife who was there with the bairns one Sunday afternoon, sitting on the beach, became like dementit and was taken pity on by the women nearby. He was blue. And also there were pictures of lions eating women, who were quite bare too, and suchlike.

To think that God could have created the bodies of women. And then one was not allowed to think about them. Maybe one was allowed to think, given that it was not a mortal sin for which one would burn without hope.

I do not know why I say all this. I do not know why I told her all those stories about Furtenback. I must have been nervous. But I do know that I almost went dementit when she said it.

She walked back home through the snow in full daylight.

She had talked and talked, but of course there was no advice I could give her. What could I say. I was not Johannes, nor Captain Nemo, and the Son of Man kept away as usual and besides he might tell on her to God. Why did she speak to me about it. Not to Johannes, not to the Enemy, not to Josefina, but just to me. And the only only guilt that could be allotted to me, I said to myself afterwards, was that I had sawn down the elk watchtower.

That night after all, I lifted up my heart to the Son of Man, but as usual he had no time for me, and must have been busy being merciful to others in this world. Then I lifted up my heart to the Benefactor, who had shown mercy to the wretched and wrecked on Franklin Island off the coast of Nyland: Captain Nemo.

And Captain Nemo had the time. It was typical. He came to me in the night and spoke to me, calmly and consolingly.

You sweetie, you, said Captain Nemo, you must calm down. God has not got to know about it yet and the Son of Man is short of time because he sits and picks at the wound in his side so it opens up for everyone who want to crawl therein. But no one can take Eeva-Lisa away from you. She is in the greatest misery, and now you must become her benefactor.

But then what about the generally well-liked centre-half from Västra, I said, the Enemy, because of course it is he, who has made Eeva-Lisa with child?

Then Captain Nemo fixed his glance somewhere in the far distance and said: I think he's travelled down south over to Ume where he has a cousin who is a colour sergeant in the Regiment. And he is considering a permanent post.

I think he cannot be bothered with her any more. And of course you cannot load this guilt on to him. You have to be her benefactor now, in her great wretchedness.

– But what about Johannes, I asked.

But Captain Nemo disappeared at that point and I was lying there shaking in bed.

If only it had not snowed so dreadfully. It was as if God was preparing for the death of the flies between the window panes. I had promised to meet her the following day.

What kind of a life is it, when the Son of Man keeps away. And Captain Nemo is completely at a loss as well.

And says that there is only me.

Eeva-Lisa had said she probably would not dare to go to chapel on Sunday, and not to the youth club on Tuesday and Friday, whatever happened. Because everyone would surely see that she had sinned.

It did not show of course. Though she may have felt it showed in her eyes.

Now, soon.

I always write that when something is very far away. Or when I am afraid of arriving.

In the library he has sometimes tried to use my hand-writing, but it is obviously him. He has prayed to Captain Nemo too. Though he was told off right and proper.

In the middle of the night, after Eeva-Lisa had been away for a few hours to tell what I already knew, Captain Nemo called on me. He was my benefactor, and I knew I should show him much gratitude.

Therefore I asked him for guidance, because I was completely at a loss.

What were we to do about Eeva-Lisa's misery, which would soon become obvious to all.

Captain Nemo had a white beard and looked elderly, the long spell of solitude in the underwater vessel had carved its marks in his face. When I had spoken my piece, he said to me:

– Johannes, it is not her suffering, but yours. You must betray her.

I then asked what kind of miserable advice this was, from a benefactor who had previously shown goodwill towards the wrecked settlers on Franklin Island. He then said there are only three kinds of people: executioners, victims and traitors. I asked which I was. But he replied that he would not reveal the answer. I started greeting then. He had a white beard and was my benefactor, but I was certain he had sentenced me to enact the role of traitor. I said that at least I was no meanie like Judas. He then replied that traitors are human too, the body has got many limbs, the hand cannot be the eye, the weak need the strong but it is also that without the weak parts the body would die, and traitors must be defended as if they were frogs. How could he say all this, I did not want to be sentenced to treachery. Still, he went on, with his sad and wonderfully otherwise smile, you are not only a traitor, but an executioner too, and a victim. I wept and said, then am I everything.

Yes, was his answer, like every human being you are everything.

There is always the hope of a miracle.

One would not be human without hope. And I surely must be some kind of human being.

3

THE EVENT IN THE
WOODSHED

Eeva-Lisa, big sister, was found
  one night in the cold woodshed.
She was ever so still and sad then,
  like a fish in a bowl, frozen dead.

I

Around eight o'clock on the evening of 3 December Eeva-Lisa came to my house and wanted to speak to me in the lobby.

It turned out that Josefina had noticed something. Why, she had not said at first. But she had understood something and so she had been told. This, briefly, was the point of Eeva-Lisa's story, which was not easy to tell. Not that brief either.

Johannes lied quite a lot, I realize that now as I add things up.

Actually, much of what he left behind in the library

was neither evasions nor lies. Metaphors, rather, like the parables in the Bible, like those used by the Son of Man when he was too frightened of God, who would punish him if he told it like it was.

Though Jesus was probably not lying or frightened after all. I used to think he was like Johannes, when I knew I had to defend things.

Sometimes it is important to defend things other than frogs.

Afterwards it could be read any way one liked: a lot of figures of speech, and a small kernel of truth, which he baked in like pieces of fried bacon in a dumpling.

It must be cut, opened up.

He has written down a story of how Eeva-Lisa had stolen ten pence, and how awful it was; it was much later when I first realized what he was trying to hide.

They had, all three of them, had to kneel in front of the kitchen sofa, and sign a hymn, and then pray together to God that he might show mercy towards them so that the contagion of sin would not affect the innocent son.

The contagion of sin was the ten-penny piece. Her taking it, that is.

But it was not that simple. He presumably wrote down a parable about the kneeling down in front of the sofa, the parable of the stolen ten-penny piece, and it would be about old Mum in the green house, and her unreasonable hatred of Eeva-Lisa.

So that the contagion of sin should not spread.

No, it was hardly that simple. That is the problem with everything in Captain Nemo's library, it is full of metaphors. I discovered that in the end.

'Library'. 'Signal'. Words which were all metaphors. That must have been why he dared leave the parables to me. Who would perhaps understand, but never ever dare tell.

I never forgave her for exchanging me. Or for what she did to Eeva-Lisa.

But maybe it is that I wipe out everything else about her, everything that could have been an explanation. Wipe it away, so that she becomes all simple and white and invisible; as if written with the index finger in the snow and then wiped away with the hand.

I imagined that she had written *you sweetie, you* to me in the snow, as if she had been a lumberjack killed by a tree, a message wiped away by the surviving benefactors. So it was wiped away for Josefina and so she was wiped away.

How could she answer, when I did not realize what the question was.

People told of how she come back home with the late bus in the evening the night Dad died; I was only six months old at the time, and so of course do not remember.

They put her off at the woodplaning plant; it was March, late in the evening and the snow was still deep, and the driver, it was Marklin, had turned towards the rear of the bus and asked if there was no one who could show her some charity. But she had not wanted that. And so she had walked through the snow, up towards the edge of the forest where the green house was.

The house was dark.

163

The immense first step into the long loneliness: as if the dizzying step into vast empty space.

Since she knew what it was to be left behind, how could she leave me behind.

But then, I might have asked.

II

She had called him and Eeva-Lisa into the kitchen, she had sat them down on the kitchen sofa and pulled out a chair and sat down opposite them, and started the interrogation.

It had become known to her, through Selma Lindgren as it happened, that Eeva-Lisa had been seen in the company of a well-liked centre-half from Västra Hjoggböle, who was said to have left the village in order to take up work in Umeå and now lived at Teg, and that they had been smooching secretly but that they had nevertheless been seen, and now she asked Eeva-Lisa if it was true, and if the lad could add anything and if he knew. Before four pairs of eyes, and that fourth pair belonged to God, she insisted on an honest answer. She had, she stressed, taken Eeva-Lisa into her house and shown charity to an orphan girl, whose mother was known to be lewd. She had no charity to spare for lewdness. She had not wanted that brought into her house. Never.

He had not dared to say a word himself, and Eeva-Lisa had clammed up, as if she were angry or baffled, and then Josefina had repeated the question if she and the lad from Vastra had been smooching.

Then Eeva-Lisa had just said

– We have no been smooching.

Once more she had repeated her question, in the sight

of the Lord, had they been smooching. And Eeva-Lisa had repeated her answer:

– We have no been smooching.

It seemed as if she was more angry about the word than anything.

Then the question was, did Eeva-Lisa call Selma Lindgren a liar. In which case Selma might be called in as a witness. And Eeva-Lisa had opened her mouth, as if to yet again state that they had no been smooching, since it seemed to be just that word which she did not like, but then she shut her mouth and said nothing at all, neither about Selma Lindgren nor about the matter of smooching. But in the end she had finally said

– Seemingly, it is all over now.

Then they had sat there in silence, thinking over the meaning of all this. And then Mum had turned to Johannes and asked if he had known. She apparently required no further enlightenment about the smooching. Smooching there had been even if Eeva-Lisa did not like the word.

After all this there had been silence for a while. And it was then Johannes spoke. He said it straight out into the deathly silent kitchen:

– But she told me that she was with child.

The silence lasted for a long time, as if after an angel's trumpet blast. Mum had stared stonily first at Johannes, then at Eeva-Lisa. Child. That meant whoring. Eeva-Lisa did not add anything about lies or false accusations. And it was then Mum had started weeping.

How could he say that. How could he. How could he.

Eeva-Lisa had just been sitting there, she had become quite otherwise, as always when baffled or gripped by despair, perhaps she had not heard what he said? Afterwards he thought that perhaps she had not heard. But no. The kitchen in the green house was large of course, like all farmhouse kitchens, but not that large. It was normal, only the colour of the house was odd. He had said it quite distinctly.

After the trumpet blast had died away, Eeva-Lisa had turned towards him, as if now when it was too late she was going to ask for his help, or to be spared, or as if she had not really grasped it.

But of course he had already spoken.

Looking at him did not help. But she had such kind brown eyes, and she was his big sister, and played with him. And I am certain he loved her so dreadfully much. And yet he said it.

If only he had bitten off his tongue and thrown it into the corner like a scrap from the slaughter. If only he had taken the knife and cut out that cursit tongue.

If only he had not said it.

I suppose he loved her dreadfully much, and was jealous, or hated her, because she had left him behind. Or something.

One always tries to invent something when it is too late. And it has already been said.

But he had not cut out his tongue of course. And it had led him into temptation.

And then he said it.

It must have been love. It is the only explanation I have. And Josefina started weeping.

Nobody could remember her weeping before.

Apart from that time when they put her off at the

woodplaner's and the driver, it was Marklin, had turned round and asked if no one would show the mistress charity. Though she had not wanted it.

But at other times: nocht.

There was no knowing what she thought. Perhaps she did not think at all. Rather, things fitted together for her. And it was not always necessary to think things through to make them fit. Enough to know how it had been. No need to think it through.

She must have fitted together things like how Dad had deaded though he was so young, and how she had come back with the bus and Marklin had turned round and said that about showing charity, though she did not want it. And surely felt ashamed about greeting that dreadfully in the bus. And then there was the deep snow when she walked up towards the green house that night. And the blacked-out green house. It belonged where it was, though it was so newly built, with the rowan as a lucky tree, planted just at the foot of the fire escape, which Dad had nailed on in case something happened. And then her first child, lying in the womb for two days the wrong way round, while she screamed like a madwoman, and the midwife had work in Långviken and did not come. And was girning when she did come (she had spoken of this). And in the end it had been too late; but the corpse had been baptized and given the same name as I was, later on (so in my life I carried a corpse-name).

They had a corpse-picture taken, when he was in his coffin, he looked like an applecore; it was somehow as if I was lying there, but it was he who died and I who was later rejected by her. Like a three-legged calf.

She fitted this together.

I am not trying to shift the blame from her. I am just saying that this is how she fitted everything together, because this is how people do fit things together. And the exchange of me for Johannes was fitted together. And she probably felt ashamed when she was with me because she had not wanted me, puir laddie. She must also have fitted in that, although Johannes was so bonnie, it was not all as she had hoped it to be after the exchange. She must have been straining all the time to think what joy it was to get back her own son, who had been lost, who had strayed but been found again, because the Bible said so. And of course to think that he was her only true child.

But it did not feel right after all.

Sometimes I believe that she secretly liked me, though I was not as bonnie and likeable as Johannes. Why should one actually need to be beautiful and likeable. She must have thought that after all I had somehow got curled up inside the wound in the side of the Son of Man. And every time she tried to hide there, full of grief over everything that had been lost, there I was.

That must have been why her face got so weird, like a raisin, when she caught sight of me later on.

Today I believe that was how she thought. But I could not ask at the time.

So she fitted it together. Fitted it together in just a second, that quick awful second when Johannes said that Eeva-Lisa had told him she was with child.

It makes one freeze over. She froze over. But why, nobody knows for sure.

It had been dreadful to see her weep.

Some people weep all the time, and of course for them it is natural. But not for her.

Weeping was not common in our village. It was not something one did. That was why hearing about the tears and the blood of the Bridegroom in chapel was so much liked.

It might have been better the other way round. What I mean is: if Jesus had held it in and the people in the village had grat.

After she had stopped weeping, and started holding back as usual, she had told them to kneel in front of the sofa.

Johannes to her right, Eeva-Lisa to her left.

And then she had led them in prayer.

It was just how he described it later, in the library. Only the tone was lying, as I noticed when picking up his defensive piece tonight. In one sense true, but the tone was false. And it was the wrong sin. It was all wrong. A slightly humorous tone, in order to bake in the treachery, like the fried bacon in the dumpling.

Yes, she actually wept; not false crocodile tears but real ones from grief or worry or strain. And her tears upset me in a special way as if at the same time I wanted to console her in her grief and to give a dull cry of protest against the tears and prayers and hymn-singing and stillness in the kitchen. As the tears kept running down her cheeks she carried on praying, ever more eagerly, as if in her derangement she was trying to assure the Almighty God that in this green house we never never never ever had been thievish or laid claim to someone else's property or stole siller. Dear Lord Jesus, she

169

continued after a short break to recover, look to us all
in your goodness, look upon them that waste away in
this world of sin and are in meesery, tak the haun of
this lass Eeva-Lisa and lead her on the recht way so
that she gets not like the loons that trauchle alang the
road and pull their shoon and live in sin. Ye ken dear
Jesus that the seed of sin has been sown in her hert
and let not the sin from her Eeva-Lisa infeck the
innocent bairns. Yes she wept, partly from grief over
Eeva-Lisa and her thieving, partly from worry and
anxiety that the seed of sin would be carried by the
wind, from this young but already spoiled grain of
wheat to her own child and that evil would take root
in him. And so she intoned: And Lord Jesus, you the
Saver of all the world hae to help so nane o' the
contagion of sin spread tae him, Johannes, dear Jesus
hae surely been so guid as to see tae it that he will no
be like her Eeva-Lisa. For the sake of the blood, Amen.

But that was not how it was. She had not stolen a ten-
penny piece. She had not stolen at all. She was with child.
And in that night she had been betrayed by Johannes.
Mum wept. But it was not like that.

It was not like that. She prayed, that is true. And she
sang a hymn, 'I am a Guest and Stranger', maybe in
desperation.

But it was he who had betrayed Eeva-Lisa.

She prayed, that is true.

With fervently closed eyes, as if her wish was that the
inner darkness would become so impenetrable that suddenly
it would be forced to fragment. By a ray of mercy going

170

through the darkness. This immense darkness, perhaps worse than anything she had experienced when she took that first step out into the dizzying loneliness the night when the bus had stopped at the woodplaner's and the driver, it was Marklin, had asked would no one show her charity, could that darkness be penetrated by the holy mercy shown to all sinners by the Son of Man?

Could she be delivered from all that had been fitted together, which now finally had been joined to the child which, she was terrified to realize, was growing in Eeva-Lisa's body, and who in turn would become a sibling of the three children she herself had lost.

The first, born as a corpse, baptized as a body but never alive. The second, Johannes, who got a name she had not been allowed to choose, but which ought to have been mine. And I, who got the corpse-child's name. Three wretched siblings, and now a fourth.

Yet one more child to be added to the line of the lost ones.

In the darkness of the night he went into the larder and cut a piece off the sugar-loaf. Then he went to the kitchen sofa where Eeva-Lisa slept.

The moon shone on the snow. The fall of snow had ceased. Snowlight as bright as day. She had not gone to sleep.

Her eyes dark. They were steadily fixed on him. She breathed soundlessly, as if she slept, but her eyes were open. He reached out with his hand, held out the piece of cut sugar for her. He waited for a long time. Her lips were dry, a little bitten. And he hoped that at last, almost imperceptibly, her lips would part, and with the very tip of her tongue she would touch, cautiously, the harsh white surface of the sugar-lump.

But she did not touch.

I imagine him standing at the bedroom window that night, looking out over the valley.

Moonlight, immensely white, the valley laden with snow. Absolute silence, no singing of a heavenly harp. In front of the window the rowan, which was a lucky tree, full of snow and berries, but no birds.

III

Christmas came.

I heard nothing from them. She did not come.

Around one o'clock, the night between 4 and 5 January there was a tap on the kitchen window at Sven Hedman's: I was lying directly below the window and woke straight away, though the tapping was very faint.

At first I understood nothing. Then the tapping came again, and I got up and looked out.

It was the winter when the moonlight followed after the immense fall of snow. About fifteen degrees under, and moonlight. Sven Hedman slept alone in the parlour. I could hear him in his sleep.

I looked out through the window. It was Eeva-Lisa. She was wearing a sheepskin coat but was bareheaded. I opened the lobby door cautiously and asked what was the matter. She squeezed herself in through the chink without saying a word and sat down in the coldlobby. I closed the outer door, and the kitchen door as well. She sat on the floor and stared up at me.

She had brought some snow in with her.

– There is sumthing wrong, she said. I have pains in the stomach.

I crept back in and put on my fleecyboots and Sven Hedman's cagoul. His heavy snores could be heard from the parlour. I had noticed that she was not wearing mitts, so I brought some, they were the ones without a trigger-finger. Her eyes were closed, and she was in pain.

What could I do.

You must help me, she whispered. I dare no be home.

She had sought me out, not Johannes. She had turned to me to be rescued.

Captain Nemo had prepared me, one of the previous nights, by telling me the parable of the visit to the very last child.

This child was alone in the whole world. All his relatives and all his friends had been taken away. Snow had fallen for a long time and covered everything with whiteness. There was no one on earth except this child. Alfhild Hedman was dead, Sven Hedman was dead, the bus, driven by Marklin, had stopped for ever, no post arrived, the green house stood empty. Everybody had been rooted out. In the whole world only one child had been left behind. That was me. I was the very last child.

Then the very last child hears a knock on the window.

Vapour came from her mouth, her head and hands were bare when she came, I got Sven Hedman's fur bonnet down from the nail too and put it on her head. She was not to catch cold, I whispered.

It was a coldlobby. We whispered.

When she felt the pains she was silent, and when the pains went away she whispered, though I signed to her not to speak.

This was not the way I had imagined it: that she would come to my house, with kind eyes and something that troubled her and I would reflect and then see my way through to the answer. Of course I had a well-thought-out plan for it all. She was to sit on the sofa and have a glass of small beer and a slice of sweet bap and a sugardoddle, which I would cut for her. And I would sit down, quite naturally, next to her and first stroke the sleeve of tulip material soothingly and talk to her quietly as a benefactor should. I would explain to her how things were. Fitting them together. And she would listen to me attentively, and now and then nod her head causing a strand of blackhair to move and her to push it back thoughtfully. And her small cat's head would be turned a little towards me, though she would be looking at the log-basket. And now and then she would speak a little. But I was to shake my head and respond, kindly, almost humorously, and this would be followed by a moment of thoughtful silence and then she would respond, with a kind of small smile. And I would nod and think about it, for what she had said would have been quite sensible, thought not without flaws, and then respond with something that was both keen and bonnily expressed. And she would look at me and laugh a little.

And so we would sit there and speak and speak. This must have been how I imagined love to be.

But since she hurt so much that she almost whimpered,

174

and was sitting on the floor with Sven Hedman's fur bonnet on her head, it did not happen like that.

The spasms sometimes shook Eeva-Lisa's body, she opened her mouth but did not call out.

In between the times when she hurt she whispered a lot. It was about what her Christmas had been like. It had not been a jolly time. It had been quite silent. The day before Christmas Eve something had happened, and afterwards everything had become quite silent. Apparently she had not said a single word for a month. Neither had the other two.

Johannes had spent most of the time upstairs in the bedroom though it was so very cold. He said that he wanted to read from the *Bible for Children*, but that is an unlikely story. Presumably he just sat there looking through the window at the falling snow. Eeva-Lisa had not gone up. She did not want to talk to him. Then I asked why she wanted to talk to me. And then she said it was because of the tulips. And I had more or less guessed that anyway, but could not feel happy about it this time.

Still, she said it. It would have been nice to find a humorous reply then, but nothing came to mind. And she started whimpering again, quietly, almost like a pig. And I made no answer.

And then we heard that Sven Hedman was awake.

He had stopped snoring. He was moving around in there, and I heard him creaking out of the bed and crossing the floor and opening the parlour door. Then silence. There was a faint whimper from Eeva-Lisa, and I put my hand over her mouth. She looked up at me then, and whimpered more faintly, though I was holding on; so I pressed a bit harder. Then she was silent.

I heard him groping his way through the kitchen, it was dark but a little moonlight showed the way to the pissbucket. Maybe he would not look on the kitchen sofa. It would all be over if he did.

Then we heard him piss in the bucket.

Eeva-Lisa looked at me but stayed quiet. This was not how I had imagined love.

He kept pissing for a long time though in sploits and muttered a bit. Then there was a sigh, and he went back and closed the door. He never put the light on.

Since then I have thought that if I had asked him to help, everything would have been otherwise. But I did not. It was because that night I was the very last person in the world, everyone else had been taken away, Sven Hedman too had been taken, the sounds were misleading. The world was empty. I was alone, and there were no benefactors, only me.

Then there had been a knock on the window, and that was how it should be, it was Eeva-Lisa. Those who do not exist cannot be asked to help when there is only one child left in the world and Eeva-Lisa is tapping on the window.

Still covering her mouth with my hand, I said:

– If you go on making a noise like that we have to go to the woodshed. Or he will hear us.

She nodded, so I took my hand away from her mouth. She pulled herself up, a little, and started sobbing again, though quietly. Then she stopped sobbing.

Cautiously we opened the front door.

I walked ahead of her. My mouth was exploring the hand I had pressed to her mouth. It was still moist. It did not taste of anything in particular.

I thought it was like kissing her and that could have been quite nice.

IV

For many years I thought of how Johannes had betrayed her more than I thought of anything else.

It is strange. But not that bad. But I suppose it made me calmer to think like that. Then the rest could be put to the side.

Executioners, victims and traitors. It was just a matter of holding on to what hurt least. What a life.

The snow had not been cleared round the woodshed. I got cold snow inside my fleecyboots, but sort of ploughed a track for her.

We never had much wood at Sven Hedman's, so I knew the shed would be half empty and in any case there would be plenty of room round the chopping-block. The hasp had stuck with the cold, but my hands were bare and I pulled it free. She was greeting more now.

I took her arm and made her sit down on the chopping-block. She looked peculiar in the sheepskin coat and the winter warmitts without triggerfingers with Sven Hedman's fur bonnet pushed down over her head. Over the woodshed door, which I had closed, was a window divided into four panes; the moon was powerful and the whole woodshed was lit almost like day though it was night-time and the light was more blue than outside in the snow.

When just afterwards she felt the pains again she did not want to sit on the chopping-block and lay down on the floor instead. The wood chips had frozen.

I had cut that day in the morning, so I put a log under her head, it was birch which was easy to cut in the cold. The log was surely hard, but Sven Hedman's fur bonnet must have been something soft for her head to rest on.

There was no way to stop her greeting. She said she was afraid of dying, but I assured her that no, never.

I had thought so much about how it could have been between Eeva-Lisa and me. I had pondered it often and fitted it together in my mind.

Of course, she was six years older than I, but that need not have been a hindrance. Birger Häggmark had married an old one, much more so, there were twenty-two years between, but the auldwife had been even-tempered and he had grat at the funeral, though of course they never had any children. That stood to reason. It must be that when something has got rooted in someone's head, the way Eeva-Lisa seemed to be in mine, then nothing mattered any more.

It would be the way it was when I sat next to her and she taught me to knit. And I would say things, not just about tulips, but things like that about the tulips. And she would say that we were like brother and sister, but it should be much more, and six years was no matter. She would never be secret with me about anything, and I would never be afraid of her.

What little did take place was like that. Not that it was much. We were never afraid of each other. But all that was left was a little saliva from her mouth, after I covered it and she was in pain. It almost froze on the way to the woodshed.

She had not wanted to taste the piece of cut sugar.

The handle to the woodshed door was freezed.

We were taught never to touch a freezed doorhandle with the tongue. Then what happened to Göran Sundberg from Innervik would happen to us, one could hear when he spoke even today. They said it was a lesson for him.

To be given a lesson was to be punished. One would just about become mute. Touching the cold iron with the tip of the tongue was almost like heresy.

Though Alfhild did sing in chapel in spite of being mute.

Outside the brightness of the moon almost roared.

The moon hammered on the window, there was a pattern of checks on the floor. Four checks which moved towards Eeva-Lisa. After an hour, when she had been quite calm, they had almost reached her. She kept lying down and would not sit on the chopping-block and when I tried to lift she threshed about. The moonlight finally reached her. Then she said she had started to bleed.

It was running down her leg, I could see it. It was clear the sheepskin coat was going to waste, but oddly enough I minded not. And I said nothing about it.

She told me what to do.

I went out, went over to the privy, which was plainly built and stood on its own, and got the newspapers. It was the *Norrie*. When I got back – I had left the door half open – she was sitting up, her back against the chopping-block and her hand held between her legs. Right up at the top. She looked scared. That was understandable. She was just sixteen years old at the time. I pulled a few pages from the *Norrie* and bunched them up, and did not even bother to save the page with Popeye, I was that scared. She tried to get the wads of newspaper in between her legs, but did not quite have the strength and just toppled head over heels backwards pushing the chopping-block so it almost fell over.

Then she just lay there and told me I maun do it.

At first I did not want to. But it was pressing, she insisted.

I tried to mop up along her long johns, but she whimpered and mewled and I must have been a bit shy, but she told me not to mind, I had to stop the bluid. She said I was to put the bouls of paper into the longjohns. But I just mopped and mopped and threw the bluidy bouls on the pile of logs without minding that the newly cut wood might go to waste. And then I gave up and leaned back against the wall and just about fanted awa'.

And then she said I had to get more paper or she would die and she did no want to die, she said that many times. And so I got more paper.

She held open the top hem of her longjohns. The sheepskin coat was yanked open and the skirt pulled up of course and I screwed up my eyes hard and pushed a large boul of paper between her legs but never touched the skin. She was overcome then and just lay there for a bit, without saying a single word though I said sweetie and would she say something. She could nairraly breathe. But when I listened I realized that she was breathing, though you had to listen up close.

Just then she found it hard to keep her food down and some ended up on the sheepskin coat.

Sven Hedman's fur bonnet had fallen off. I put it away so it would not get stains.

I think time must have passed.

Not a long time, but the moon had moved, you could tell from the rectangles on the floor. The window was not in the door, of course, so though the door was half open the window openings were fixed. The moonlight had passed over her body and was moving now over towards the newly cut wood.

She had scratched a little drifting snow together in her hand, and wiped herself with it. It was red.

Outside the wind had got up a little. The dawn was coming, so it became much darker, the snow was drifting and coming in through the open door. The door banged and rattled, I tried to close it but it was hard. My hands were quite damp of course and I almost stuck to the cold iron but did not mind, though I knew there was a lesson to be learned if one stuck and froze and had to tear free, but it was not worth thinking about now. The house was dark. Sven Hedman must still be asleep. Please let him not get up for a piss, I thought, then he might look at the kitchen sofa and not find me on it. He pissed every night, many times. I was quite alone with Eeva-Lisa of course and Captain Nemo was really to blame for giving me the notion that I should not call for help, because he had told the story of the child who is alone in the world when there is a knock on the window. So there was no one I could ask for help and support, and in spite of that I was afraid that he would get up for a piss and find that I was not there in my bed.

And then.

What I mean is: then he would light the lamp. And look around. And see the tracks to the woodshed.

What would we do then. In that case we would be at an utter loss.

I had stopped thinking 'I' and was thinking 'we' instead. Though it was not nice and jolly the way I had dreamt it would be. Before, I was the one who was at a loss about what to do, now it was 'we', but the wrong kind of we. But something had happened anyway, I felt that.

Eeva-Lisa sat up and opened the waistband of the long-johns and had a look.

She looked quite dreadful.

She began talking, but as if she had become half dementit. There was no sense in what she said. She started talking about her Mum, not her in the green house, though she had already been told, on the second day, to call her Mum, but her own Mum. Whom I had not heard her speak of or mention before. There was something about her Mum having sinned by playing the piano, and also having been lewd, and now the contagion of sin was spreading to her children and her children's children, and her Mum had had to go to South America and got Parkinson's and been eaten by rats while she was just lying there. It was all completely confused. Most of it she seemed to have dreamt. Though it was more like a nightmare. But even so she seemed to ramble on about her Mum as if she had liked her, although she had never seen her. Of course it is usual that people in emergencies start to like Mums and Dads they have never seen, so I understood and paid no attention to her blethering. But then she started on about how she had sinned and how God would punish her, by sending a fish into her belly, the fish was biting her now. She had been refused the right to a real child because she had been whoring. And the fish bit her, and the puir fish must be bashed to death against the railing of the boat. She kept talking about this fish until I was fit to scream. But then she got all overcome again and fell over forwards into the bluidy chips next to the chopping-block, and I almost had to throw myself at her again, so she would not hurt herself. And straighten her up. And make her lie back again.

I kept my haun against her cheek, and she became a bit calmer.

The fish came now, she said suddenly. He bit.

And then I understood.

Of course, I was not a child. What I mean is, of course I was. But I had been there when calves were born, and pigs, and pulled heifers along to the bull-keeper and been around at the slaughter. That is village life. So one is not just a child.

I had seen blood and afterbirth, so has every child who grew up the way I did. It was natural, nothing to remark on or pay attention to.

But never like this. And then it was Eeva-Lisa as well.

I realized of course that it was bad. It had not gone to term. What could I say: she might have been in the sixth month. This was no ordinary calf, but Eeva-Lisa's child, and I liked her so much it was practically a mortal sin, and she was about to die in my arms. And no one must know. She said that all the time. She insisted on it, though she did not speak clearly. And I had to swear before the Almighty God; at first I did not want to but she became quite contrary, and so I swore not to call Sven Hedman in the parlour of the house there.

The longjohns were sodden now.

I went over to get a couple more copies of the *Norrie*, because the others had been used up. The custom was for water to be boiled when a child entered into this world. But there was no water. I thought that snow was water too of course.

But how could I get rid of all this blood and slather before dawn, when Sven Hedman finished snoring and got up for his coffee and morning snuff.

She must not to die in my hauns.

I thought: If she dies in my hauns this night then I shall die with her. It was a resolution. She is not to leave me behind. Johannes had betrayed her, but I stood by her, and she must not leave me. That was my resolution.

It was dead when it arrived. It certainly was. If it had not been, she would have asked me to save it from suffering, such was the state she was in. But it was quite dead. But slimie, like the fish before it is bashed against the railing of the boat.

But she did not ask for it. I state this before God, who like a coward keeps himself to himself until Judgement Day when he is to master us wretches, and before the Son of Man, who is always too busy when he is really needed.

Afterwards I also spoke a lot about this to Captain Nemo, my benefactor, who was with us in our misery and shall be for ever.

Something had happened the day before Christmas Eve in the green house.

Josefina had been standing at the top of the stairs, with Eeva-Lisa in the middle and Johannes at the bottom. And she had begun quite calmly by saying that she had arranged it so that Eeva-Lisa was to move to Erik Öberg's, he was the cousin of Öberg the dentist, and so that was that. But bit by bit she had begun howling that she had forgiven this whoring in her own house, before the Almighty God she had forgiven the whoring even though it was a hard thing to do, and she had been all twisted up, but Eeva-Lisa's silence, that she could not stand. Nor her hatred. She could bear the whoring, and forgive, but not the hatred and that nobody spoke to her although she was the Mum, and then she had said something about Eeva-Lisa and Johannes which was a lie and just a sign of how deranged she had become.

Johannes had been standing at the bottom. But absolutely the only single thing he could remember afterwards, was not any of the important things, or the lies about him and Eeva-Lisa. Only that now Eeva-Lisa would be taken away from him, and that he was a traitor.

He had not been able to say anything, though there was nothing wrong with his tongue. And Josefina had been laying down the law and greeting a lot, which made it worse still. And nobody had shown her charity.

It had been a silent Christmas because of all this.

She cannot really have believed that Eeva-Lisa was with child. That is how it seems to me. Because if so surely she would not have.

I am certain of this. The rest of her screaming was only

quite natural lies, which I shall never ever repeat, nor will Johannes, not even in the form of a parable.

There was nothing else for it but to pull down the bluidy longjohns and help her.

A child had come out, though it was rather small. And of course it was dead, I can swear to that.

I no longer minded anything. I took the child in my bare hands and looked at it. It looked bonnie, a bit like Eeva-Lisa, though it was smeary and dead. It was a wee deadboy. I felt somehow solemn. Perhaps one does when it is all over.

Eeva-Lisa was ill and raving, but begged me fervently to hide the child in the depths of the lake. I promised her to do this. I wrapped the child in a couple of copies of the *Norrie*, and walked through the deep snow down towards the lake.

It would get light about eleven that day. The moon had disappeared. I buttoned the sheepskin coat around her before I left and held my hand against her cheek for a while. Outside it had become so dark it had to be morning.

4

THE DEPTHS OF THE
LAKE

White moonlight on beautiful snow,
    all the children God will see right.
Perhaps He will care for fishes too,
    caught in the mesh of moonlight.

I

It was heavy going in the deep snow. The lights were on
at Nordmarks, but elsewhere the village was dark. At first
there was a drip from the parcel, but then the dripping
stopped.

It was drifting. I padded through the deep snow down
towards the lake with my brother wrapped in the *Norrie*.

When something happens and one has not yet understood
that nothing is hopeless, it is like being deaf. Nothing can
be heard so it must be that no one is talking. The deaf ear
is all there is to rely on. The loneliness is absolute, however

many voices there might be, calling out around the lost one.

Quite silent. What is there to hear then.

But there is always something better on offer than death.

The lake was rather long: it got narrower in the middle, then opened out, and farthest away, so far away it could scarcely be seen, was the marsh with Ryss Island.

The ice was thick but the inlet was running and still open. There was always open water in the winter.

The edges of the ice were yellow and it smelt of rotten eggs near the open water. The current was so strong one could see it.

I was tired and peched like an auldhorse when I got there, though my burden had been light and I had not pulled anything. I had steeled myself, and stopped greeting. The edge of the ice used to be weak and we were always told not to go close and Eeva-Lisa was sitting in the woodshed waiting for me, so it mattered that I should not fall in.

It was important not to drown yet.

I took the last steps cautiously and looked about.

It was dark, no moon and no stars, though the snow shed a light. The song of the stars was finished for ever for me, the depths of the lake lay ahead. I unwrapped the *Norrie* round the parcel and looked at it. So it was a boy.

This was not very good.

I looked up towards the village so that I would feel better, it was almost so I could not keep my food down, like Eeva-Lisa when just a while ago it had got on to the sheepskin coat, but after some time I could look out again over the current gap in the inlet.

It was just a matter of calming down. And so without looking I wrapped the parcel again, it was just as well. Now it had to be thrown.

Then I threw him. The question is, what would he have been called.

The parcel floated for a while, quite a short while. After that it slowly began to sink. Then the paper unfolded and stayed on the surface, drifting in the light current towards the edge of the ice on the lakeside. It stayed there, floating.

The boy was no more to be seen.

I did not know what to do. If someone came here they would be sure to ask themselves what the *Norrie* was doing in the water.

The pages were bloody as well. But who would come here.

I could not go out there and get it, I might well go through the ice. And Eeva-Lisa was waiting for me, it was important not to drown.

The boy had sunk. He was drifting with the current for sure, slowly on his way towards Ryss Island maybe, where the dead Russians were buried, and where there were snakes. Maybe he would drift all the way to the Mela River, where Alfhild Hedman once had become a horse, though she died later.

His eyes had been wide open when he was lying in the *Norrie*. Now he drifted under the ice, slowly and almost thoughtfully, with wide-open eyes, I thought. Quite slowly.

The question is what did he see.

Perhaps the Son of Man would show him mercy. He was meant to be the children's friend, even if he had no time for me. One could only hope that he would show mercy towards Eeva-Lisa too, and maybe me, though we were alive.

Then I went back.

II

Sven Hedman had seen me from the kitchen window and came out on the steps and asked.

I did not answer, I just went into the woodshed.

Eeva-Lisa was still propped up against the chopping-block, just as she was when I left. Her eyes were wide open but she did not look at me. I asked, but she did not answer. I went up to her and felt her cheek.

She was sweating, but quite cold.

– Eeva-Lisa, I said. I am here. Sweetie, Sven Hedman is standing on the steps, calling out. Soon he will be here, it is the morning, Eeva-Lisa.

She just kept looking straight ahead.

There is so much said about miracles, but hardly anyone is a believer. It is thought to be just something people say. But it is not something just said, it *is*. And even when it seems things could not be worse, nothing is entirely without hope.

And because of this, miracles exist. It must be understood, though it took me a long time to grasp it. My whole life in fact.

I held my hand to her cheek, and then I took it away. Then Eeva-Lisa said:

– Do not tak your haun awa'.

190

And then I put my haun back again.

She said: I know you have done what I asked, I am very grateful to you for that. Now I must tell you something. How do you know I have done what you asked, I replied. I know, she said. I know that you are afraid, but you must not be afraid any more, because I am not afraid. All that is finished. Now you must trust me. You must trust everything that I tell you, or it will be bad for both you and me. What am I to trust, what are you going to say, Eeva-Lisa, I responded. I am going away for some time, she said, but there is nothing to worry about, I will come back to you, I will return. What do you mean, I said. I shall not be leaving you behind, she said. I must die for a while, but it is not the way they think, because I will come back. Will you be leaving me behind, I said. No, she said, and it is not that I am coming back in heaven, it is here on earth. Keep your haun there.

I could not feel sweat any more. She was quite cold. I kept my haun there.

– You believe, she said, that the worst has happened. But everything is still about to happen, the most important things. What is to come now is the worst and the best, keep your haun there, now you really must listen to what I say. I will go away for a time, but I shall not leave you behind and then I shall faithfully stay at your side during this life on earth. You are not to think that I mean heaven. I will come back here. What blethers, I said, it cannot be, it is not possible. Keep your haun there, and then I shall tell you the secret, she said. What is the secret, I said. It is that I am dead but will shortly rise again, and return to this life on earth. What blethers, I said, and started greeting again, it is not possible. Now I have told you the secret, she said, I shall say no more, because I have told you everything just the way it is. Now you must go and get Sven Hedman.

She was so bonnie. But she said no more. Just sat there, propped up silently against the chopping-block, looking straight ahead with her browneyes. What was it she had said. How could I believe it. But then I thought I had better believe in her promise to come back to me.

And so I took my haun away. And I went to fetch Sven Hedman.

IV

RISING FROM THE
DEAD

1

THE MYSTERIOUS ISLAND

I

The signals and the signs not clear.

The sleeping birds had sat themselves down in strange formations on the lake: they had lain down on the white cover of snow and together created signs, or letters, as if on their way to form words.

That they were failing to do so was very obvious in the first days after the event in the woodshed. I watched them without telling anyone.

They were going to arrange themselves into a signal, but were not yet able to.

Sven Hedman scrubbed the woodshed. I had been sent off to the cottage hospital, but since I was perfectly well I was allowed to return the very same day. Mostly, I sat at the kitchen window, and kept an alert watch on the signs, without a single word or gesture to reveal to my friends that perhaps the Benefactor intended to use a signal for my guidance.

They believed they were burying her in the cemetery in Bureå on the Saturday of 9 January 1945. It was thought unnecessary for me to attend. Only a small handful of relatives followed her to the grave. Nobody mourned her.

Her half-brother from Finland had telephoned but did not come.

Sven Hedman had been there and to distract me told me what it had been like. Apparently, everybody thought that she had passed away. Nobody had any idea that she was to rise again, and return to me already in this life on earth. When Sven Hedman had been sitting there for some time, cracking awa' about it over the porridge cap, a flat dish poured full of cold rye-flour porridge with a butterwell in the middle out of which we both ate with a spoon from each side of the table, and to be kind he finished his half before the butterwell so that I should have the guidwell in the middle to ease me. For a while I considered revealing the secret, but decided it was not necessary and stayed silent.

The vicar, who was known in the whole parish for being solemn but not very quick on the uptake, had performed the burial service. Forsberg was the preacher of the Trust, but he dug graves to support his brood of seven children, and did not take the bus to the villages when he was preaching, because they nairraly had food for the poor bairns on the mean wages of a preacher, Forsberg had done the digging. In the winter that meant using the pick for ever. It was hard shovelling for the poor lass from Sjön, he had said at the meeting in Västra the following week after he had led them in a prayer for the dead on behalf of the poor lass from Sjön. Everyone had understood that this about hard shovelling was a metaphor, and Hildur Östman had grat at this point.

He had not led the prayer for the dead in Sjön, something everybody found odd, but then he had got his own ideas of course. He had been to the school for preachers in Johanneslund on the outskirts of Stockholm, and although he had not, and this was said with certainty, been damaged by Stockholm ways, he still had notions of his own.

The vicar had done the burial, but it was Forsberg who had done the digging.

The village was talking. That was perfectly natural.

They must have been trying to figure it out. There was the blood of course. The deadboy was never found, and thus his existence could only be guessed at. The Sheriff had been, but had not wanted to go far out in the deep snow and the ice edge was weak of course. So the investigation had been interrupted.

Things were being thought through. But the secret was not known.

I divulged nothing of what had happened, because I had been given no guidance by Captain Nemo and from the signs I realized that he was not yet ready.

Sven Hedman had put the maps of Sweden which Alfhild had drawn on greaseproof paper in a pile in the shit-house, but they had not been used.

I went through the maps carefully. They appeared nondescript, just clumsy outlines but with Hjoggböle marked to calm her.

However it was a matter of not being duped. Damp had

197

damaged many of the maps in such a way that a certain pattern could be distinguished, made up of the mouldy holes and patches.

Captain Nemo seemed to be getting ready to send a signal through to tell me what to do. Something was up. That much was obvious. But since the map was partly destroyed, or had to be regarded in a special way, the message was not easy to interpret.

Some more time passed. What was I to do.

Sven Hedman often asked, but since I did not know the answers I kept quiet. I had received no guidance. One day the vicar arrived. They kept trying for two hours. But nothing was caught on that fishing trip. The thaw started, the deep snow was soaked up into the soil. I went back to school, because that was held to be necessary. But nothing was said about what had happened to Eeva-Lisa. Everybody spoke of her as if she were dead and I to blame: they prayed for me once at the youth club. The vicar called again and was solemn. This time he wanted to talk to me face to face and spoke severely, as if to frighten me. In order to hide that I was waiting for guidance from Captain Nemo I told a few funny stories about Furtenback instead. The vicar looked at me as if he were a pillar of salt, and wanted to know why I told him this but nothing about Eeva-Lisa. I answered nocht. He stared at me then as if I was dementit, and left. That was the last time he came asking.

On the eve of the first of May there was no bonfire.

On 27 May 1945 I went to chapel for the first time. It was Forsberg. They all looked at me quite a lot. Josefina was there with her young son.

That was when the signal finally arrived.

Captain Nemo appeared before me, just while I was watching the Saviour in the picture with the chipped frame. Captain Nemo was in hurry, almost sweating, it was while they were singing of 'O Sacred Head Sore Wounded', but he had a short message which could not be misunderstood.

He said to me: You must attempt to find the deadboy, so that through him you can contact Eeva-Lisa, who is waiting to rise again. Ye're dementit, I said, scared, but so nobody could hear me, how am I to find him again. Then he said: Take Johannes with you to help. You must find Franklin Island. The answer to the riddle is there. Where is Franklin Island then, I asked all perplexed.

But he had disappeared.

Nobody noticed what had happened during the guileless singing of 'O Sacred Head'. I did not let on. I gave Johannes sidelong glances. Did I really have to accept help from a Judas like him?

But still.

On the way out from chapel I walked behind Johannes. I went up to him and said: We will find the mysterious island again, there you will get to hear what happened.

He looked at me as if I had gone dementit. Then he nodded and asked me in a whisper: Where is the island? It must be in the lake, I whispered. I think it is Ryss Island, but we will have to explore. How can we explore, he said. We have no boat.

We had no boat.

I said: We will have to make one.

Then Josefina got him away from me by pulling him abruptly by the arm.

That evening I scanned Alfhild's maps carefully. The mouldy patches on the greaseproof paper looked like birds on yellow ice. If they were stacked one on top of the other the result was a new map. I knew I was close to the answer.

The following day I signalled Johannes by waving when he was standing at Sehlstedt's byre, across the valley. He stood there as if dropped from the clouds. But he must have understood, because after a while he made a sign back which I could quickly interpret.

It meant: in the volcanic crater on Franklin Island.

II

A great river ran through the lake.

It entered by the northern end of the lake and left by the southern. The river came from far away up in Lapp country and in the spring it was used for floating timber. That was exciting and you could watch it from inside the part called the Lake, which was not the part called the Marsh.

Towards the end of May the lake could been seen slowly filling with cut timber, blocks of ice and drifting ice-floes, the timber sometimes getting stuck along the shores, in the north mostly at Ryss Island but also around the outlet. And later on, around midsummer, it would all have gone at last.

But not all the logs. The stuck ones were still there. These tended to be the best wood, floating nice and high. The sunken logs were those with too much water in them, soaking it up and then sinking, it was the same with people, preacher Bryggman had explained at the Army of Hope.

Some floated down to the sea, but some stuck and some sank.

I knew what happened to the stuck logs. After a week

200

the lumberjacks would arrive, prod the logs away from the shores, pull them together into a train and send them on their way to follow the rest. The lumberjacks walked along the shores, and then rowed out in boats: they could clear the shores in a day, and then the whole lot was gone.

The last timbers were called 'the leavings'. And when the leavings were gone the lake was empty again.

I had no boat. But Captain Nemo had given me guidance and strength. I would build a boat. It had to be a raft. Then Johannes would help me to search. He was a Judas-wretch and a traitor. But Captain Nemo had given the order.

I had been ordered, during the singing of 'O Sacred Head Sore Wounded'. So this is what I did.

I hid three logs before the leavings went.

On Sunday 3 June, during the hour before the midday service, I went to the Mela River. I chose Sunday because I wanted to be left in peace: at that time everyone was in chapel. Besides I thought chapel unnecessary.

It had got so that the Son of Man busied himself doing other things and never had time for me. The Son of Man ought to help at the worst times. He is meant to be a benefactor and to intercede. But he had not. Captain Nemo had. But the Son of Man: nocht.

Attempt to find, Captain Nemo had said. So I built a raft.

First find the deadboy. Then Eeva-Lisa would rise again in this life on earth. The deadboy had surely drifted under the ice and got stuck, like a wee log. Stranded on a strand. Such was the nature of floating things.

The leavings had not gone. There was plenty of timber. The water was high, it went far up into the ditches.

I slaved all day. I pulled three logs up into a ditch, so they should not be discovered and be taken off with the leavings. It was heavy. I prayed for a bit to Jesus Christ, but there was no word in reply, so there was nothing for it but to carry on without him.

I was in a frenzy. There was plenty of auldgrass. I covered up. Now it was just a matter of waiting. When it was time to build I would order Johannes. He would not refuse, because Captain Nemo had decided that his will was mine.

I was hiding in the forest the day the leavings went. They noticed nothing. Now it was time to build the vessel which would take me back to Eeva-Lisa.

As a child, I often pondered what Johannes was really like.

It is very perplexing. What one is like oneself is hard enough to know. What one is supposed to be is worse. When I was a child I wanted to be like Johannes, but I was like me. That was the hard part.

Johannes was quick, and could speak fast when he wanted to. He was nimble-witted and went about in the village and was generally well liked. When he ran in his canvas shoes he was the fastest. When it came to digging a machine-gun nest in the sand quarry he was never scared it would cave in. When Eriksson's cat had jumped for the fishhook and it bit into its mouth and it had screamed so awfy he had jumped at cattie and pulled out the hook. Everybody else, especially me, had just been standing about oogling. He had fallen asleep once in the chapel and no one had minded. When five kilos of bananas arrived in

Koppra, though he had no money he had bought three before anyone else got a word in, and had been praised by Josefina. Nobody could have guessed there would be bananas in. But he was that quick-witted.

He got everything right. I had never told him that he was a Judas-wretch. But after all that with the Enemy and Eeva-Lisa he became scared of me. I was the only one who knew, and the one who knows is worth being close to and keeping in well with.

So he obeyed when I told him about Franklin cave. No questions asked. But when one is exchanged the way we had been, then you have something in common. One is exchanged from, the other one exchanged to. But exchanged. It is like seeing double.

I told him what to do. And he obeyed, that June day when the leavings had gone.

Every day the signals became ever more clear.

I stopped speaking altogether, to husband my strength. I held my leg in the burn, the leech came swimming up and settled, but did not suck my blood. She just settled on my leg, with a movement like a hand patting a horse's muzzle.

It was all so clear. I watched her with a smile of confirmation. She swam on her way without a word.

III

We pulled the logs out into the water, placed the longest one in the middle and the others on either side, and put cross-boards over them. Right in front there was one cross-board which we hammered into the logs, three boards in the middle, and three more right at the back. We used six-inch nails, except right at the back, where we tacked down with three-inch ones.

I said, rather loudly:

– When we do not need the raft any more we will break loose the boards and pull out the nails. If we leave the nails in, the saw blade could be destroyed and that destroys the piece-work rates for the lads. The piece-work rates must be a consideration.

Johannes did not reply, as if he had not listened properly.

I thought it was well said. He would never have thought of the nailsawing.

I went on to explain, because beginning to explain had worked so well. I explained that it was important that the raft should be able to carry us both. I knew I weighed fifty-two kilos. He presumably weighed about the same. The raft would have to carry well over one hundred kilos then, but the timber was dry and floated high.

He made no remarks about all this.

I had thought of the equipment as well. The provisions were kept in Sven Hedman's sandwich-box, which I had taken. They consisted of: one bottle water, one piece sausage (ten cms long), one half loaf, eight ship's biscuits, one knife, one hundred gms margerine, twenty lumps sugar, one small jar of molasses (a kind of darker syrup which was given to the cows but was just as good and cheaper than syrup, so thought Sven Hedman), four pieces flat-bread. Those were the provisions. I had written it all down in the notebook, in order from top to bottom, like a salvage list.

I had done everything on my own. Johannes had not done anything. That was probably why he was so silent.

We set out at seven in the evening.

It was as if he had become otherwise of late.

Before he was keen to make the decisions, he was the one who was quick and bonnie and generally well liked.

But now. It was contrary. He was getting more and more like me. It was as if he was beginning to join up with me. Dreadful, if one thinks about it.

I thought I ought to tell him this.

It was windy and we had rigged up a sail on the raft. We had stuck a sheet between two poles, which we had braced with string. Sometimes when there was a gust of wind, as there sometimes was, we held on to the poles ourselves.

The wind was blowing straight out from land, from the south, that is from the forest with the clearing where Alfhild had become a horse and walked round and round the stake and they had come to get her. The wind blew from there. The question is could I, I mean we, have acted any other way. We could have taken her away from Brattbygard and from the crocodile man and from him with two heads and from where it was smelling worse than the pig-house. But that we had not done.

One must not ponder such matters all the time.

That is where the wind blew from, I have thought about that since. Things cannot be assumed to have meaning, but often do. It is hard to keep up. 'Signal', as Johannes used to write in the library. He meant that attention must always be paid to the signals.

The sun was shining at an angle, nicely. We were blown along.

That spring I often thought of the deadboy.

That is to say, Eeva-Lisa's. In bed, when just lying there almost asleep and before real midnight when Captain Nemo came along to put things right, sometimes it was as if the deadboy I had carried wrapped in the *Norrie* that night had been connected to the lives of the other deadbairns. As if it was he who had been born cord-strangled, and got my name, or I his. As if it had been the same deadboy.

This was not how I thought the night when it happened. Then I just did what Eeva-Lisa told me. But just at the funeral, when Johannes did not dare be there, and I was, but I must get this right, because I knew of course that Eeva-Lisa was to come back to me in this life on earth, it was then Josefina Marklund, I thought of her as 'Mum', though I had been told off by the vicar after the exchange, then Mum had looked at me. Right across the shovelled, it was done by preacher Forsberg, as it happens.

She had just looked and looked. And then I thought: That deadboy, Godalmighty. I did not say it though. But Godalmighty, the deadboy. Imagine, she may really have wanted Eva-Lisa's deadboy. Maybe she liked bastards as well. Why else take Eeva-Lisa in to join us.

But since that night when she came back from the cottage hospital, and the bus had stopped, and the driver, it was Marklin, had turned and asked if no one would show charity towards the mistress, since that time it would not have been possible to have children except bastards and changelings. Or something.

And then, at the funeral, she looked at me across the shovelled up. It was as if she wanted to say: I could have cared for the poor lad, if I had known.

Poor lad. Though of course only I knew that it was a boy I had carried inside the *Norrie*. Imagine if she had wanted the deadbairn in the *Norrie*, if she could.

When I thought about that it got almost solemn. Like it was when I unwrapped the *Norrie* and looked at him. It was almost solemn then.

Captain Nemo himself had said, one night when he came to me and I asked why she had yelled at Eeva-Lisa from the top of the staircase, that she had to go, he had said with his calm, somewhat thoughtful expression that he could well understand that.

It was not wickedness, but love.

He said that although he had not entirely understood all I was brooding about, he could understand that sometimes I had bad dreams about the deadboy in the *Norrie*. And about how he was floating under the ice with wide open eyes. Once he himself had felt just like that. In response to my question he gave a detailed account of a situation which of course I recognized from the book. But I surely had not realized how it upset Captain Nemo.

He had been standing at the glass-pane in *Nautilus* and watched the woman and the child from the English frigate he had sunk sliding down through the water. Practically smiling as they drowned. Captain Nemo said he knew just how ill it might feel. Of course he was the one who had given the order to attack. The child, who could have been about six months old, had floated through the water, carried by a deepwater current.

Was it the same then with the deadboy in the *Norrie*, I had asked. Yes, Captain Nemo had responded calmly. So surely the deadboy too had been carried under the ice by the current. Far far away, towards Ryss Island. He rose and fell and looked up through the ice which was grey underneath. And as he rose he bumped against the ice, like *Nautilus* at the North Pole, which besides was a situation which Captain Nemo had mastered only with the greatest difficulty.

Captain Nemo knew what it was like, he said.

That is the way with the real benefactors. They have the experience.

IV

What are we looking for, Johannes said again and again.

I did not answer, it was unnecessary.

We searched along the western shores that evening. The wind dropped, I punted with a fenspost I had cleverly brought along.

I did not say why we searched. It was rather quiet aboard the raft.

Towards morning – it had never been dark of course, the wind had died down around eleven – towards morning I got cold. There were of course no houses here along the northern edge of the marsh, there were houses by the inlet and Forsen and Östra and Västra but not here. I was quite calm, not worried that we would be seen, and Sven Hedman was certain to think we were sleeping over at the Mela River hut. I was cold, but there were barns just about everywhere.

We moored. I took the sandwich-box provisions with

me, though Johannes said he wanted nocht and it was beyond me to urge him.

We went into the barn. The raft was moored.

The auldhay was furthest in. Most of it had been taken. Neither of us could sleep. And I took Johannes to task.

He had, I told him, never shown any charity towards a single soul. Nairraly a single one but himsel'. The only thing he had seen was Mum standing up there on the staircase, screaming, but did he know what her face looked like? Had he listened to Marklin, the driver, when he asked if nobody had any charity? He had watched her hardening, but not softened her. Had he thought of nothing else but running swiftly in canvas shoes in the summer and in fleecyboots on the hard snow in the winter and being bonnie and generally well liked.

And Eeva-Lisa.

I told him of the night in the woodshed.

Johannes had buried himself deep in the auldhay. Of course, I had always wanted someone like a brother to tell everything, or someone like Eeva-Lisa to love so very much and her to love me so very much that we could sit speaking for a whole evening. But all I got was someone silently burying himself in the auldhay. And Eeva-Lisa had passed on, admittedly only to come back again in this life on earth, but she was taking her time and the Benefactor was the only one I could ask for advice, but where did that get me. Sometimes it was not enough.

I felt wrathful. Johannes buried himself in the auldhay and kept silent.

Having to feel wrathful, what kind of a life is that.

I think he fell asleep.

I listened to his calm breathing and thought how nice it would have been if it had been Eeva-Lisa. Imagined that she had had the boy after all and that he had lived. Then she would have been sitting with him held against the dress with the tulips, the ones which grew downwards, and as smooth as skin and the deadboy would have been snoozing and sleeping and been well, and I would just have been sitting there calmly, watching. Such was my image of love.

Towards morning the wind began blowing from the east, it came suddenly and harshly and there were almost white horses.

And then I made up my mind.

I woke Johannes with a movement of the hand. He woke up at once, as if lying there on the look-out. He smiled at me a little, as if knowing what I had decided, and nodded, as if understanding.

Then all at once it became so nice. One makes up one's mind and then one's mind is made up. And you have only to carry out what was decided, and Johannes and I were as one, though actually it was so very difficult.

We went down to the lakeshore. We cast off the raft. We poled out.

Johannes placed himself up front and I stood away at the back punting with the fenspost. The sheet was up. There was a stiff wind, but the marsh was not that deep so I could reach down with the fenspost, we got far out right away, the sun was in the sky though it was night, but it was in order of course, and it is hard to remember exactly how it happened. It cannot be true that I had decided, why should I not then remember what happened? I do remember what happened. Ryss Island was straight ahead. His feet were bare and he stood there on the timber. I had not told him to stand. The water washed over the timber though it was floating high, I kept one foot on Sven Hedman's sandwich-box, to stop it from being washed away.

He did not wear shoes. It must have been slimie on the timmer. I did not jolt with the fenspost, besides I remember for sure that it had got so deep I could not reach. So I jolted with the fenspost, it was slimie on the timmer, he was not wearing shoes, he waved his arms about and then he fell.

And I clearly remember his face in the water then, I saw how he was both scared and ashamed of having been so clumsy, it was as if he wanted to apologize. The waves were quite high. I saw his face in the water, just before he vanished under the raft, and I clearly remember how I reached out with my hand to Johannes my best friend, as if to save him in the greatest danger, but at that very moment he was dragged down into the whirling waters, just as big as the Flood when it sucked the almost unclad women into the vast watterhole.

The next thing I remember must have been hours later.

I was sitting right at the back of the raft. It had been blown up on to the beach.

It was on Ryss Island.

I knew exactly what it was like, in spite of never having been there. Most people thought it was about one hundred metres in diameter, covered with a dense old forest of fir trees, with branches unbelievably long and strong, and that it was full of adders and dead Russians. But nobody had been there, nobody in the whole village.

And it was here I had to search. It was here.

Johannes was sitting curled up right at the front of the raft. He had pulled himself out. But he did not say anything and I knew something had happened.

– Johannes, I said. Do not be cross because I did not get you out.

It must have been overcast, I remember it was very hazy, not dark but murky, the way some cloudy nights are. He had got himself back up on the raft, though I did not want it.

– If only you had drowned, I said in a low voice.

He did not answer. But after a while he got up, jumped from stone to stone, walked through the shore-reeds and on to land. Strangely, he was wearing fleecyboots. I thought for a few seconds that I must be dreaming, but I heard the sounds very clearly as he was splashing through the shallow water, and dreams do not have sounds.

He walked inland. Ryss Island was very small, that is well known. Maybe a hundred metres in diameter. It would not be hard to find him again.

Strange about the fleecyboots. They flopped and made a noise as he walked towards the fir forest and vanished.

I did not know then that Ryss Island was much larger than I thought, that it was hiding something and that this would be the last time I saw Johannes for more than forty-five years. He vanished into the interior of the island I had feared all through my youth, without knowing its real name, and without knowing that one day the Benefactor would guide me into the interior of this mysterious island, where Johannes, my only friend, would wait for me. Now I was free but only for a while. I was freed of him, without knowing that I would remain his captive for ever; and that much later would I find him, in Captain Nemo's library, in the vessel, inside the innermost waterfilled crater on the volcanic island, off the Nyland coast, where only Hjoggböle was marked on the map on the mouldy grease-proof paper, which had guided my Benefactor.

V

At full break of day I spent a long time searching for him.

Before I began exploring I rehearsed carefully all I knew about the territory I was visiting. There were fir trees one hundred years old. The Russian soldiers buried there had been in the earth for one hundred and fifty years. The island was full of adders. Taken together it was all well known and I felt not the smallest chiffin of anguish.

I began by walking right across the island, then back again, then in circles, then along the beach. No grass grew under the fir trees. The ground was black or brown with old needles. I walked round and round, calling his name, Johannes. I shouted and begged him to show himself.

He was not on the island.

I walked back to the raft. I felt hungry, got hold of Sven Hedman's sandwich-box where I kept the provisions and opened it. I had put the molasses in a jam-jar. I opened the jar and ate some with my finger.

I got it on my face. I did not bother washing. Briefly I felt distracktit, but steeled myself. I was not cold. I knew that Johannes had vanished, he had left me behind on the island, he too. I ate the molasses. I had been left behind.

That afternoon the wind died down and the lake was glassy.

I was perfectly calm, but wondered why Captain Nemo did not come when I invoked him.

Could he have become like the Son of Man? No, I dismissed the thought.

In the water-mirror I could see that it was me it reflected back. It was quite definitely me, though the molasses had turned black round my mouth and cheeks. I did not want to wash.

I called out to Captain Nemo once more, now in a loud voice, almost as if I had become impatient or frenzied, but understood that summer afternoons were not his best time. He probably slept during the day. He was my benefactor at night instead; but I would have been pleased if he could have advised me all the same.

The fir trees were easy to climb. The branches came well down and were immensely thick, almost like tree trunks, they were like the fingers of God, thick and reaching out in all directions to punish. I climbed up and out along one of them. The finger of God did not tremble. I held on to an upper finger to stop myself from slipping, and listened astonished to the rustling. I could walk some three, four metres out on the branch, and could see far away then.

Two boats were seen rowing northwards. There were faint shouts.

I sat down on the branch until they disappeared from sight. They were still searching the shores.

What was I to do with the raft. Maybe they would see it.

I climbed down, went to the raft and took down the sheet-sail. I walked through water, felt no tiredness. I was filled with the strength of God's fingers.

I hid the raft among the reeds. They would not land. And they would not find the raft.

The clouds disappeared in a light haze, the sun was low. I soaked three of the ship's biscuits in the water. After eating my provisions I lay down on the fir needles and looked upwards.

I tried to make what had taken place add up, but could not. It is unbelievable how Mum on the staircase could have come out with this lie about Johannes and Eeva-Lisa. If he had been close by me I would have comforted him. But he had left me. Captain Nemo, whom I once more invoked, suddenly arrived for a quick visit. He thought that it would soon be time. Time for what, I asked, almost impatiently. For steeling oneself, he answered. But you must find the deadboy first.

Then he disappeared. Not a word about Johannes: it was as if he had never existed.

I climbed back on to my look-out place on God's finger in the fir tree. The finger was trembling now, as if God was ashamed because Captain Nemo had time to give advice but not his son. The sun was low. Four rowing-boats were within sight now, all on their way towards the inner part of the lake.

They were like the cows. They were trudging back to the byre. I saw them disappear down the narrow strait, then they were gone.

God's finger stopped trembling then. I pondered what Captain Nemo had told me. I sat down under the tree. It must be that way.

It must have been close to midnight when I found it.

The sun had gone down, the watterie mist hung over the lake.

I was calm and collected.

Three times I had circled the shores before I found the deadboy. I had been right. He had been floating under the ice and got stuck on the shores of Ryss Island. Captain Nemo had guided my thoughts. Though after all I had mostly been doing my own thinking.

I recognized him. At first he looked like a skelton of a pike, picked clean. But looking closer, it was quite obvious. He was held fast, almost impossible to discover, a bit up on the land between two stones. He must have been pushed up when the ice broke. Only the whitebones left, but the head was gnawed nicely clean. One imagines it will look dreadful. But it was quite clean and nice and bonnie, like a small white bone-dolly. Then I called Captain Nemo, but he did not come. So I bent over and picked up Eeva-Lisa's deadboy.

I washed him at the edge of the lake.

I went and got the sandwich-box. I pushed the sausage furthest into the corner, then the half loaf, the biscuits, the flat-bread, then the water bottle, then the margarine in its paper. There were twelve lumps of sugar left. Then the knife. Then the resealed jam-jar with the remaining molasses. Then I took the deadboy and put him carefully in the empty space on the other side of the sandwich-box.

I pushed the food back so he was quite comfortable. Then I closed the lid and tightened the strap.

It was ready.

I pushed the raft out from under its coverings. I put

the sandwich-box right in front, where Johannes had been sitting. I poled out. The fenspost was my only oar.

It was very solemn, I punted through the watterie mist, I was very calm. Johannes had left me and I had found the deadboy and everything was as it ought to be.

I landed at Tunnudden, where Sanfrid Renström had once put the shit-tuns so near the edge of the lake that the water had reached them and carried them off, so he had to row out and get them back in the boat and was then shamed generally. He was dead now. I stepped on land with the sandwich-box and pushed the raft out and away.

I stood for a while watching it slip further and further away and finally vanish in the mist. They were sure to find it. Then they would search, but not find. Then they would break up the raft and pull the nails out and send the timber down south.

And no one would know.

I picked up the sandwich-box with the provisions and the deadboy inside by its strap and walked up through the forest. I did not notice that my feet were bare. It did not hurt. The path was soft. The pines were kind and rustled yellow and bonnie. I felt happy and grateful to my benefactor, who had guided me and given me advice.

The molasses felt stiff on my face. I then walked all the way up to the cave of the dead cats, carrying the sandwich-box.

2

THE CAVE OF THE DEAD CATS

I

Tonight, sorting through Johannes's messages from Captain Nemo's library.

He is toying with my names, as if that made any difference. He has drawn a line through my name, next he calls me by another one. It is the third time he changes me.

Ashamed, I suppose.

There is snow tonight, quickly gone in the rain. I miss the light winter nights up there. The lightness of the winter nights stays in the memory.

And the northern lights. Where did everything actually go.

I visited the cave of the dead cats again this May 1990.

Benshill is still there, the forest too, but it is different in a wrong way. Travelled back to the airport afterwards. Made a brief note: 'Everything is otherwise'.

The cave was smaller, it seemed somehow constricted.

The hill was not so high. Nothing to be found in the cave either, not even the once quite clean skelton of a cat.

It shrinks out of my grasp.

Why does it shrink. If I do not hurry, it will finally cease to exist.

Must hurry before it all shrinks away. It is probably rather like adding up.

II

I walked, sandwich-box in hand, all the way up to the cave of the dead cats without a single soul seeing me.

It was the very end of the night, the sun was coming in almost on the level through the entrance and the cave was quite light.

I sat down fast by the cat skelton, it was a catgirl's. She sat quite calmly leaning back against the stonewall, as if it were a chopping-block to lean back on.

People think of course that skeltons are ugly but they are really quite bonnie.

She was sitting there, looking out over the valley. One could see it through the cave-mouth. Had she been able to speak we could have exchanged a few words, but it stands to reason, there is no talking to a skelton. She might not have much to say anyway. And what could I have asked about.

A lot, come to think of it.

In my thoughts I called out to Captain Nemo, but he paid no attention to my calling, no time I suppose. I waited for a small chiffin of time. The sun moved over the cave floor, then I called out to him again but realized I had to wait.

The valley was how it always had been. I grat a bit, but became calm afterwards. I could see part of the still lake, but not Ryss Island with the volcano in the middle, whose entrance I was later to find, and where *Nautilus* was. There was no smoke visible. This must be the reason why nobody in the village had guessed. If smoke had been coming out of the aperture, everyone would have found their way there, full of reverence, including the local press, and it would have been in the *Norrie*.

I sat down next to the catgirl. I too sat there, propped up against the wall of the cave. The catgirl had been sleeping like this for many years. This must be what it is like to be dead. Nothing simpler.

It must be harder to rise again. Better ask advice about that.

I slept for a while.

No one came to me in my dreams. I called out to No one again, but he must have been busy. I thought, one gets a knock but nothing is hopeless, I used to think that, I slept more calmly then and found it easier to steel myself.

The sandwich-box I had not opened.

When I woke the sun had moved across the floor. It was like a clock, almost like the moonlight on the floor in the woodshed which reminded me that time was passing. I did not mind much any more about clock time. It was Something. It was always there. Every day at the same time it mimicked itself. You had to be careful to remember that something had happened after all even though the clock stayed the same.

It was such a good thing that I had the sandwich-box. The food was in there, the provisions, that is, which would save me in my misery. And I had the other thing too.

Perhaps it should be taken out.

I woke up, and there was bad singing in my head, I was quite at a loss for a short while and so I began at once to think through how the green house was built.

I went through the house so to speak, so it would not vanish if I needed it in an emergency. I thought of how one could walk through the house, how it was built and furnished, and a lot about the upstairs bedroom. I found a twig and drew the groundplan, like a map, and also marked where the fire-escape had been put under the bedroom window, the one on the gable end, before putting in the rowan, which was a lucky tree and where there were snow and birds in the winter. Then I drew a coarse outline of Sweden all around, so that the house was in the right place.

After just a short while everything felt good again. It is often like that, nothing is hopeless. One must know what to do while waiting for the Benefactor.

After drawing and feeling good it became unpleasant again, but only for a quite short time.

I decided without further ado to unpack the sandwich-box.

The leather strap was not at all hard to undo, there was a clasp on it, that was only usual.

I took the lid off. Now it was a matter of arranging the salvaged things in a purposeful manner. In a really bad situation, Captain Nemo had taught me in a previous conversation, correct and sensible planning could save lives. So, I took out the ship's biscuits and placed them on a dry branch, to keep them dry. There were five left now. The knife was put next to them. The margarine to the left, starting from the catgirl, then the flat bread, which after a moment's hesitation I decided to place on the branch next to the ship's biscuits. The water bottle. The sausage. The loaf. The sugar-lumps. The margarine was close by.

The jar with molasses, which belonged among the most precious of the things I had salvaged, ended the row of resources.

Then it got unpleasant again, but I steeled myself and stopped greeting quite soon. One must always steel oneself.

The question was where to put the deadboy.

Once more I repeated to myself the reasons which made Captain Nemo otherwise, compared to the Son of Man for example.

The Son of Man of course had the wound in his side, from which came blood and water, and one could crawl into it. But unlike Captain Nemo, he had never shown that he could be properly trusted, when misery was at the door, say.

I held this against the Son of Man. Not an easy thing to say straight out, but he could not really be trusted.

Somehow, he had too many to care for. All the time one had a feeling that when times were very bad, somebody else might be having an even worse time.

And then one was left behind of course.

From this point of view the Son of Man did not quite stand the test. If someone is left behind, a real wretch, maybe, how can the wretches still trust him afterwards.

Like the frogs they have been pailed out of the cold spring, with no one at all to defend them.

This was the most important difference. In the case of Captain Nemo now, the thing was, I had more and more come to look to him for safety at those times of wretchedness when the Son of Man was otherwise engaged and not defending the poor pailed-out ones.

Those were the reasons. I recalled all the reasons and when I tested them I found they were true.

Of course the deadboy could stay inside Sven Hedman's sandwich-box, there was nothing against that.

It was empty of provisions now. If he was left inside, it would be like the corpse-pictures on top of the best chest of drawers in the parlour and quite bonnie in its own way. But since my stay in the cave of the dead cats might last for a long time perhaps it was not proper.

There was a difference between being proper and not: the same difference as between what is bonnie and what is not.

That is why I lifted the deadboy out of Sven Hedman's sandwich-box carefully, with my bare hands. He was quite dry and nice. A whole spring in the lake had passed and now he had dried out.

I went over to the back wall of the cave and put him down next to the catgirl. He was smaller than she, almost. They looked quite nice and bonnie the two of them. With their emptyeyes they watched the valley, where the water of the lake could be seen but not Ryss Island where the large fir trees grew with branches as thick as God's fingers, not trembling at first, but later when I heard the shouts from the search boats, they had started trembling as if God had got scared.

One could think about that for a while. Before I could never have imagined that God was scared but that time the fingers had shivered, like Elma Markström's hands. She was shakhanded.

In a way, it was likeable that God was scared.

The boy said nothing, neither did the catgirl. What could they say. For a start it is always hard to mak' up sumthing to say. Secondly they were both dead. But neither of them looked evil.

I took a ship's biscuit, broke it, dipped a piece in the molasses and jokingly held it out towards the catgirl's mouth. She did not move. I kept my hands still. She did not taste it.

I did not dare to offer the ship's biscuit to the deadboy as well. I ate it myself. It felt nice now. The dreadful came on again sometimes, but briefly. Then it went.

I felt better when I had eaten the ship's biscuit. There were only four left now.

If I had had a notebook and a pencil I could have written a salvage list, or a verse, but I had no notebook and no pencil.

The sun had stopped moving across the floor.

I sat down at the mouth of the cave and looked out over the valley.

Shouting could be heard from down at the lake. Then there was no more shouting.

At about midnight Captain Nemo visited me.

I had fallen asleep when I heard a whisper which made me wide awake at once. Someone whispered my name. The surprise somehow made me open my eyes wide, but no one was to be seen in the cave. I looked carefully at the catgirl then and at the deadboy at her side; the deadboy had slipped over to the side, just a chiffin, as if he wanted to lean against her. It looked rather odd.

Only them and me. The deadboy belonged to the family somehow, to put it that way, but I had never thought that about the catgirl. Not before. But when the deadboy leaned over a chiffin it became easy to think like that. In a way they were sitting there chatting.

Just then I heard the whisper again, and this time it was louder. There was no mistaking it. It came from the deadboy. He said to me:

– Ye hae tae gae oot. He's oot thar. He's bidin' on ye.

– Fit's that ye're sayin'? I responded then.

– Ye're no tae gae trachlin' thar, ye hae tae gae oot, the deadboy repeated in a rather sharp tone.

It was baffling. Somehow one became quite baffled, almost upset, like the time Egon Backström had fallen asleep in chapel and burped whilst he slept and did not have the sense to pray for God's forgiveness in the youth club the following Friday. I realized of course that the deadboy could not speak, partly because he had been dead for a long time, and partly because he had never learnt to speak, because he had never been born.

I must have gone dementit then.

It was not only all this which made me so distracktit. What upset me most was not that he was speaking even though he was not allowed to because he was dead, but that he addressed me in such a coarse, almost rude dialect. At secondary school we were not allowed to speak like fair-mers, we had learnt proper talk there, but the deadboy had never gone to school.

Then I considered. There was no need to feel bad. At that moment I mesel had of course answered in the same dialect, without considering.

I looked at the pair by the rock wall for a long time.

They stayed perfectly silent. Slowly my upset died away. But long after my upset had died down I could still feel my heart beating and beating. I realized that I had dreamt, and in the dream he had spoken to me, in coarse dialect; I had dreamt evil, but I was not dementit yet.

Jokingly I threw a small stone at the deadboy. I hit him and he jerked, almost admonishingly, and I regretted it at once.

It was then that I grasped what he had said. Someone was waiting for me outside the mouth of the cave.

Captain Nemo was sitting outside the cave, on the right hand side, and he had been sitting there for a long time, I saw that, because when he stood up I noticed that his backside was wet from the dampness of the grass at night.

I apologized at once for the delay, but he silenced me with a movement of his hand.

The morrow had come and mist covered the valley and one could no longer watch the lake. His face was covered with mist and was the same colour. Somehow it was a solemn thing to see him.

There was something in his hand.

– Come in, I offered, but he declined with a shake of his head. He just wanted to give me a message.

We sat ourselves down on the ground.

He had been worrying about me, he explained. Rescue might take some time to come; ordinarily, perhaps he would have been able to lay down a signalling wire for me to follow on to the next message, but time would not allow it. People in the village were looking for me, but had so far searched in the wrong places. No one knew about the cave of the dead cats except the three of us, Johannes, Captain Nemo and myself. And because I could not let myself be known it was now important that I should get clothes and provisions. The weather was still fine, he explained, but the summer would come to an end, September would come, and then the cold pierced through flesh and bone.

I had to equip myself.

For what foreseeable time must I then equip myself, I asked. He did not answer the question directly, but gave me a piece of cloth he had brought with him. It was dress material. I asked how dress material was to keep out the cold during those nights when it would otherwise have pierced flesh and bone, but he seemed amused and laughed, and then he became serious again, and told me to turn the material over to show the pattern.

I did so.

To my great surprise I recognized the material with the tulips from which Eeva-Lisa once had made a dress. I asked how he had got hold of this material. I got it from Eeva-Lisa, Captain Nemo replied. Does she know where I am staying, I asked. Yes, he responded. Where is she then, I asked. That I must not tell, he answered, but she sends you greetings and begs you to trust her.

I wrapped myself in the material. Captain Nemo helped

me. We were both careful so that the flowers, they were tulips, would grow downwards.

I gave Captain Nemo an account of the situation with respect to what had been salvaged and the resources I still had.

The loaf. The ship's biscuits (now four items). The water bottle, the margarine, the knife, nine sugar-lumps and a jar of molasses, filled up to about a third. I listed the provisions and asked for advice. He thought it through and then said he supposed that I could get help from him. These new resources he explained, would be brought the following night. Until then I had to get my sustenance from what there was.

He had a few lumps of sugar and two grey dumplings in the pockets of his cagoul.

I asked where he had found the dumplings – I had never seen Captain Nemo with dumplings previously. He did not reply to this, but said he supposed that the mouldy bits on one side of the dumpling could easily be removed with the knife, which thus turned out to be useful. I asked where he would find the new resources. He answered that there was flat-bread in Alfred Sjögrens shed, and since this shed was close to the edge of the forest he intended to steal up to it silently the following night and without being seen find his way in and take the flat-bread cakes.

Are you going to steal, I asked horrified. No, he said, but you are a human being in an extreme emergency, I am your benefactor, and so I must act like this.

I must show charity towards you, he said. I nodded in agreement.

And he said: One of these nights soon I will bring

228

somebody with me, a friend of yours. One who can safe-guard you too. Who is it, I asked, is it Eeva-Lisa.

No, he answered. Another friend. But you must not ask any more now.

He rose, suddenly remembered something and put his hand in his pocket. He handed me a notebook and a pencil.

He gave me them and left. His backside was still wet.

I went into the cave with the tulip material wrapped round me. The deadboy and the catgirl were sleeping peacefully now.

I lay down on the floor of the cave, wrapped in tulips. I dreamt of the Benefactor and about the friend who, the following night or one of the following nights, would come to visit me, according to my benefactor.

III

Early the next morning I left the cave and walked over to the sawn-down elk-tower.

The floor of the platform itself, and the railing surround-ing it, were lying collapsed and partly broken up; nobody had been there to repair it or to collect the wood. I looked watchfully out over the valley down there. I could see somebody, very black and small, walking across the farm-yard at Sehlstedt's. But no boat on the lake, and nobody shouting.

The figure who had crossed Sehlstedt's yard must have been Yngve, I thought. Then I pondered over what it meant. But it was meaningless. I realized that in my present emergency, like someone ship-wrecked, it had got so that what had meant something before no longer meant anything. I realized that I had to strip away all that used to mean something before, because now the situation was quite different.

I began to break loose the one-inch boards. It was well built and I had to work very hard.

It came to mind easily that Eeva-Lisa and the Enemy had been up in this tower once. That was how the very misfortune began. But then I saw clearly that it is impossible to know when a misfortune really starts. It could have been long before, for instance when we were exchanged, or when Mum tried to pail out the frogs or something. So the elk-tower was no more guilty than anything else.

I gathered up about ten boards, and hammered the nails in with a stone. Then I carried the lot, in two trips, down to the cave of the dead cats.

I made a floor to sleep on.

It was like a bed made of boarding. It consisted of the boards from the collapsed elk-tower.

The deadboy watched me working with a very faint smile on his bonewhite face. I wish I could have read his thoughts. He could not have known where the boards came from of course, or what meaning they had, not only in my life but also in his.

I wished that he had a name.

I straightened him up and he did not mind.

There was still some seaweed on one of his legs, which were like a bird's and unlike the rest of the skelton not white. He seemed to me more restless at night than during the day.

Once he seemed to have gone, as if somehow he had left

230

his place next to the catgirl. Then I went out of the cave and called out to him. He did not answer. When I got back he was sitting there again next to the catgirl, but with a small strange smile on his lips.

So far I had not given a thought to the notebook, the last small gift from Captain Nemo.

I opened the notebook and found to my surprise that there was a verse written in it, in a strong hand, and probably with a so-called timberman's pencil. One might call it: a poem.

It said:

One tinder-box with steel and flint
One barrel ship's biscuits
Some books, paper, pens and ink
Two axes, two saws, two planes, a couple of iron bars,
    one hammer, nails and various other tools
Two complete suits
Two dozen shirts
Two guns, two sabres, two hunting knives and a pair
    of pistols
One small barrel gunpowder and a quarterweight shots
One telescope and
One roll sail-cloth

Like a statue, I stared at the verse. I did not recognize the handwriting of course, but grasped at once what Captain Nemo had given me.

It was the notebook in which my Dad had written his verses before he died.

He had written poetry with a timberman's pencil. Then he had died, when I was only six months old and Mum in the green house had returned from the cottage hospital late one night, and the driver, it was Marklin, had turned round and asked this thing about showing charity.

I had believed that the notebook had been burnt. But it had not. Dad had written a salvage list. And he had asked Captain Nemo to hand the book over to me.

I understood. I could not see how he could have realized, at that time when I was so small and had not even been exchanged, what was to happen to me. And what kind of advice I would need. But then there is so much one does not understand in an emergency.

He had written the verse with the salvage list for me, his own boy. Now Captain Nemo had brought it along. And when I understood that Dad had not left me behind, I felt all otherwise and began to greet.

I understood exactly what it meant. It was Dad's poems. He had written them for me.

The following day, in the morning, a cry woke me early.

Captain Nemo stood at the mouth of the cave and made a sign for me to come out. He had brought the flat-breads and a sheepskin. I realized he had got into the shed unseen and succeeded in his exploit.

I thanked my benefactor eagerly, but he silenced me with a movement of his hand, and then just disappeared.

I went back to my sleep. I had the impression though, just before falling asleep, that the deadboy – or the catgirl – was moaning quietly. But they did not seem to be in any way otherwise and looked straight ahead as before.

I moistened their lips with molasses, but their lips did not move and they said nothing.

232

No more sounds. The boards kept the cold away. I had spread the sheepskin over the wooden bed.

No dreams.

IV

From the top of the pine I could see that they had started cutting the leens at Sehlstedt's.

For many nights there was no Captain Nemo. The deadboy sat quite still and seemed dismissive.

What is wrong with you, I asked many times. We must stick together.

He did not answer.

But I had overlooked one of the verses in the notebook, written with timberman's pencil. It was on the last page.

I read it quite quickly, and understood nothing. Afterwards I had of course noticed that Johannes had included just that page, torn out of the notebook, in Captain Nemo's library.

It was rather poor verse. Mostly about love. Four lines, with rhymes.

It hurt terribly. He had written the salvage list to me of course, to give me a poem which would be a help in my great wretchedness. But the verse on the last page, besides it was quite poor, he had written to Mum in the green house.

She had herself confirmed that writing verses was a sin and said that she had burnt the notebook. She must have thought that Dad should not have to burn in hell for the sake of a few verses.

What hurt was that he had written to her. And in spite

of being rather a poor verse, though with rhymes, I realized that we had seen different people in her.

Now of course it is too late to look again. Often you fit things together too late. Why did Captain Nemo have to come there with the notebook, with the last page left in, when it only hurt like this. It is enough to make one frenzied just thinking about it.

When I read the verse aloud to him, Eeva-Lisa's deadboy looked straight ahead and refused to answer.

'Now we rest still together'. We? It was enough to make one dementit just imagining it.

The salvage lists in the notebook I could understand. But this was harder. He must have written it to Mum in the green house.

Because there was no one else to write to. I tried to imagine them, the way he described them then, about twenty-five years old, but I could not do it.

Bad singing started up in my head. When the singing is bad one becomes almost desperate. The person he had written about must of course have been the same one who stood on the staircase and screamed at Eeva-Lisa. Thinking about it, it meant that I and Johannes and Eeva-Lisa had never understood what she was really like.

I mean: we had left her behind. And not listened to Marklin in the bus when he turned around. Of course she was the one who needed charity. Not me.

Captain Nemo had given me the notebook with the verses. They were from Dad and were written to help me in my wretchedness. Why then did the last verse have to be there, it caused bad singing in my head.

The deadboy smiled. I became frenzied and poured a little molasses into both his eyes.

I could tell what time of day it was, but forgot to count the days.

Sehlstedt's had some twenty-six stacks visible from the top of the pine.

It got harder and harder to put up with the words and whisperings from the deadboy and the catgirl.

They pretended it was nothing, but spoke a lot between themselves. I told Captain Nemo this when he came the following night.

He pretended not to understand, but left four new dumplings which he had got from Hugo Hedman's cellar, and a litre of milk which he had got by milking on the sly the previous night. I asked him why it was so easy to sleep and so difficult to stay awake, but he did not explain.

The days were the worst. At night I dreamed a lot about being a bird locked in between the winter-pane and the summer-pane, and when I woke up I was cold.

You are running a temperature, Captain Nemo said anxiously.

I gave the deadboy some of the milk. He opened his mouth a bit and some of it got down, but most ended up outside. I think he was grateful, because in that late night he did not whisper.

What have you got against me, I asked sharply. Every-thing, everything I did for Eeva-Lisa. And she left me with the promise that she would rise again in this life on

235

earth, but she has still not come. What kind of a mother have you got.

Sharply, like the Bible, that is how I spoke to him. He just sat there with his emptyeyes full of molasses. Then I tried to whisper, with the softvoice. You sweetie you, I said, it was so dreadful to walk down to the lakebraes with you in the *Norrie* and your Mum bluided so dreadfully, I should have gone to him, Sven Hedman, and there were many people who stared at me at the funeral, as if I had taken the poor lassie's life, that is to say your Mum's, but sweetie you, she told me to take you in the *Norrie*.

He just smiled. He must have been trying, before himself and before me, to avoid the blame for what had happened. Me, or her, or Mum in the green house.

But there was not a word about the one who had betrayed her.

I wiped his eyesockets clean of molasses using the tulip material.

When the deadboy and the catgirl were silent, and Captain Nemo was busy being a benefactor to others, it got so silent that I could hear the bad singing.

But Eeva-Lisa had promised to rise again. When it was especially silent, more so than ordinary silence that is, I sat there hoping for Eeva-Lisa's rising.

V

I woke when somebody touched my arm.

It was Captain Nemo. At his side stood Mum from the green house.

You look a sight, she said in a kind way. It is the

236

molasses, I said. Take the soap and gi' yersel' a wash, she said. How did you find me again, I asked, but she did not bother to explain that.

Her eyes were all strange, all kind. I have come here to confess a sin which has weighed me down greatly and I want to be forgiven for it, she said. Is it about Eeva-Lisa, I asked. Are ye dementit, she responded, almost sharply. No, but I regret that you never got to have a cat. But the first one we had shat on the iron range and made me that angry. Now I have brought you a cat for you to keep it, while you are in such great wretchedness. Have you brought a cat, I said quite dumbfounded, and added hurriedly: Well, that with the iron range, that explains it.

I regret that I exchanged you, quite a bit, she said sort of casually. Johannes of course never really existed, she said, almost solemnly. No, I said, that is quite natural. Yes, she said but this about you not having a cat, that is the worst. Will you forgive me.

I nodded. When the firstcattie shat on the iron range then it is of course easily explained, I said. You sweetie you, ye're so bonnie, she said then. Now I have confessed my sin.

She was wearing Eeva-Lisa's tulip dress. It was quite strange, because I was lying there wrapped in the same cotton material, but neither of us thought it worth argufying about.

Here is the wee cattie then, she said. It is Eeva-Lisa. She has risen again. How come you were so angry wi' her Eeva-Lisa, I said cautiously. Weel, a' ye bairns stuck together so I was that left behind, she said severely. More than ever before, and then there was no one who showed any charity to a mistress left alone. Yes, I see, I said. Is this Eeva-Lisa.

Yea, she said and sounded kind. And now she is risen.

She looked around the cave, looked at the deadlad and the catgirl, saw the provisions and nodded assent.

Then they left. Captain Nemo had not said a single word. But the cattie stayed behind.

It was obvious straight away that it was Eeva-Lisa, though somehow it took some getting used to.

She had the same beautiful dark slanting eyes as before, and black fur, but was rather thin. How are you then, Eeva-Lisa, I asked. Nae bad, she said. It took you a long time, I said. But I have been quite far away too, she said. It was dreadful that night, I said, but I carried the deadboy down in the *Norrie*, and now I have fetched him back here. I know, she said, one must always fetch things back.

She was so wise.

I took off the dress material with the tulips growing downwards, and carefully wrapped her in it. You must sleep now, I said, and then you can tell me how everything has been. And you too, she said, must I really sleep now. You must, I said. Fancy that the fox did not get you. Yes, though it was hard sometimes, she said. I have milk, I said, I will give you some tomorrow. Now you must sleep.

I put her in the crook of my arm, her nose pointing inwards. She was so beautiful and nice. Fancy that you could rise again after all. *Mmmmm*, she said.

She fell asleep almost at once. I stroked her over the tulip material. It felt just the way I had imagined, the time when I did not dare.

For sixteen days we lived and talked together. It was how it should be. Just how I had imagined love to be. We would be sitting there speaking together, and sometimes I would stroke the tulip material with my haun, and then she would smile at me gently.

For sixteen days we were left together, and I got to say all I wanted. It is odd that still things did not add up for me. Everything was said just the way it is, and that is good. But it does not add up. That happened first when I was going through Captain Nemo's library, trying to find out how things can be also-said. First time round, things are also-said. Then a long life passes, you travel a long way, you hurt people and gets hurt yourself quite a lot. And then you can begin to add up.

But the sixteen days with Eeva-Lisa in the cave of the dead cats was a beginning after all. I think that was why she rose again and came back to me.

And the last night – I did not know then that it was the last, but it was – she said something I would think about a lot later on. I have been away, she whispered, lying there with her nose in the crook of my arm, wrapped in the tulip material the way we always did it, but I have returned. Soon I will leave you again. You must stay silent for some years, and think things through. First you thought it was impossible that someone could die and then rise again in this life on earth. But now you can see that it is possible. Now, here comes the worst part. Now is the time for you to grow up. But you must add things up. If you do not then my life, my death and my rising have been completely without meaning.

What am I to add up, I asked. You will come to understand, she said. One gets a knock, but nothing is hopeless.

That is what I came back to say. But what am I to add up then, I repeated.

She had black slanting eyes and nice fur. And she had come back. It was to take many years before I understood her answer. This is the way with those who rise again. It takes time before one can understand what they say, and why they returned.

So she told it the way it was, and I understood nothing. Then she curled up again in the crook of my arm and fell asleep, her nose up.

And however much I search through Captain Nemo's library, I can never, never find the text saying what the risen Eeva-Lisa told me that night. It cannot be written down, I have understood that. Adding things up is the only way.

They found me on 21 August 1945.

I assume they had noticed Captain Nemo at some point, stealing by with the provisions he brought me, and realized.

There were three men who found me and took me along, and there was not much to be said of course. I hardly put up any resistance, but told them that I wanted the molasses and provisions with me, and that the deadboy had to come, but that the catgirl could be left.

They put a warm sweater on me, collected the provisions, were perhaps a little perplexed by the deadboy, but wrapped him in newspaper, it was the *Norrie* again, and brought him along.

Then we left the cave of the dead cats.

The wood from the elk-tower had to stay.

Eeva-Lisa had sneaked out when they entered the cave. They did not try to catch her and I said nothing. She disappeared into the forest. She had returned as she had promised, but now she vanished into the forest of my childhood.

I know the fox is dangerous, and that the going is hard, but I know she will manage.

They took me down to the green house, before they escorted me on the way to detention.

Mum stood in the door, took my right haun, and her eyes looked bonnie again. Took my haun, and led me up to the bedroom where she put me on the bed. There, she said, I was to sleep for a while. After they had left I saw how she stood at the window, she tried to be quiet but I could hear her greeting.

Then I got up and took her haun. There we stood for a while looking out over the valley: over the rowan, and the wild-rose hedge and the cold spring with the frogs. I held her haun hard hard, because she must not be sad. And she did not take her hand away, we just stood there, until she led me back to the bed and sat there looking at me while we waited for me to fall asleep.

I said nothing and neither did she. But there was no need to say any more, everything had been said already that time when she visited me in the cave. I had forgiven her all that with the cattie, and she had forgiven me for not showing her charity, and we understood everything.

And that was how it should be.

EPILOGUE
(Starting Points)

If the enemy has not been found, then he must be recreated.

I stayed silent for four years and two months, while they observed me, and tried to make it all add up. It was not that I had nothing to say, which is what they thought. I was thinking it through.

Then, as they said, I got well. But though they thought that I had been ill, which was not the case, neither did I get well at that point, because I had not got it all to add up.

It was the salvage lists in the notebook which made me understand how to begin. I found them again, after all these years, in Captain Nemo's library.

Soon I will have gone through the library.

Not all of it, there is probably no time for that. But I have added things up and attempted to get my thinking finished.

I will never manage it, I know. But I dream sometimes, because so many years have passed since it happened, dream secret and happy dreams about how it really could be possible: not just trying to fit it all together, I really do try, but finally succeeding. And being finally able to write: it was like this, this is how it happened, this is the story.

Woke at three forty-five, the dream about the cave of the dead cats was still very much alive. Unintentionally stroked my face with a finger, against the skin of the cheek.

Had been very close to the answer.

Got up.

Out there, above the water, hung a strange morning mist: the darkness had lifted, but there was still a hovering grey cloudiness, not white but somehow reflecting darkness; it hovered a few metres above the surface of the water which was absolutely still and shiny, like mercury. The birds slept, tightly wrapped in themselves and in their dreams. Can it be that birds dream? The mist was so low that it left only water and birds to be seen, only a black unmoving surface of water, an endless sea. I could imagine myself on the outermost shore, and in front of me nothingness.

An outermost boundary. And then the birds, wrapped tightly in their dreams.

Suddenly, a movement: a bird taking off. I heard no sound, I just saw it beating the surface with the tips of its wings, free itself, rise at an angle, upwards: and it happened suddenly and so lightly, so weightlessly. I saw how it took off and rose and rose up towards the grey ceiling of mist, and vanished. And I had heard not a single sound.

I waited, but there was nothing more, absolutely nothing. Perhaps this is how it was for her that night in the woodshed, supported by the chopping-block. I believe so. Not at all as dreadful as the time she left me behind.

Just like a bird taking off and rising, which is suddenly gone, and returns, like the hands of a clock, but changed, though not in appearance.

He makes notes of the words of the code in the margin, now I can easily interpret most of them.

'The corpse-picture. Suddenly he sees himself.'

'Signal.'

I have at last accepted the spells, their existence, that is. When they are seen as spells they become easier to bear.

After his death, there was found in his pocket a notebook with poems he had written, by hand, using a timberman's pencil. It was a bit out of the ordinary, lumberjacks away up there were surely not in the habit of writing poems.

The small book was burnt at once.

I do not know why. But perhaps it is the case that poetry is sin, that art is something sinful, that he was fallen, and therefore burning was the best course. But sometimes I wonder what it contained.

So: it was burnt and it is gone. A message that never got sent. Sometimes I think that part of what I myself have tried to do must be understood as attempts to reconstruct a burnt notebook.

Not reconstruction: spells.

Maybe it was not the case that I stayed silent while I was detained.

But that I said nothing.

They found many ways of explaining me, during those years of my detention.

In the end they got to like me. There were so many explanations, and I agreed with all of them, to make them think me bonnie.

I stayed silent, but spoke vivaciously. I never spoke about the fire. But that was quite natural. It is enough to make one despair at those who do not understand that the frogs must be defended, that the Benefactor sings through the heavenly harp when the Son of Man pretends to no longer have the time, that a human being can rise again in this life on earth, and that a rowan is a lucky tree, in which there are snow and birds in the winter.

Everything is really so simple. But it took a lot of time to simplify it.

Johannes of course never rose again.

It is true of course that if someone does not exist, then he cannot die, and then he cannot rise again. He was my best friend. I wanted to be like him, although he was the traitor.

I tried to explain this to the people who detained me. But they understood nothing.

They gave me a cat, because they thought I liked cats a lot: I was to take responsibility for it, and this was to strengthen my character during my detention.

How ridiculous. On the other hand, it was really about

time too. They did not understand of course that Eeva-Lisa had escaped out into the forest of my childhood, where she was managing well and waiting.

I opened the airlocks to the ballast-tanks and went into the boat. All the lights in *Nautilus* were switched on. There in the library Johannes was lying on the kitchen sofa, looking bonnie, and was dead.

Rising can only be done on one's own, and in this life on earth. Probably that is what I finally understood. It is not any simpler than that. But who said it was meant to be simple.

The walls of Franklin cave paled slowly as the vessel sank. I sat in the aluminium boat and was quite calm.

Nautilus sank slowly through the black water, the lights got paler and paler, and in the end it was just as if faint northern lights were flickering and disappearing.

I rowed out and was free. I had to get back out there, but freed.

Sven Hedman visited me once in the detention room.

I think he liked me. He said we should have looked after Alfhild better, when she became a horse. I said nothing, but we agreed at last.

When he left he patted my muzzle as if I had been a horse too.

I should have looked after Sven Hedman better too.

Josefina, Mum in the green house, came to visit just once before she died.

She found it difficult to talk, but wanted to come back, she said, there was something she had not understood. She

249

was somehow in despair. But I thought that there was surely no cause for despair. Eeva-Lisa had come back to me. And though they thought that she had sneaked out of the cave that time, and disappeared in the forest, she had in fact stayed with me.

It was so simple, once one thought about it.

Josefina looked old when she left. She was still beautiful in some way, though she was old, and sad.

She did not understand, she said. But who had said that understanding is possible. It is not, but what would we be if we did not try.

The air is clear tonight. The stars are visible, but not the northern lights.

Where did it go.

It was like this, it happened this way, this is the whole story.